Ode to a Dead Lord

A THEO BRYGHT, RUNNER MYSTERY

JOLIE BEAUMONT

ASTER PRESS

First published 2011

Copyright © 2011 by Linda Feinberg
Cover Design: Linda Feinberg
Illustration: Fashion Plate (Walking Dress), March 1820:
Public Domain

ISBN 978-0-9837931-0-6

Published and distributed by:
Aster Press
Kansas-Jerusalem
asterpressbooks@gmail.com

PROLOGUE

The deep blue damask curtain parted, pulled aside by the tug of a heavily veined but still nimble hand. A narrow shaft of sunlight thrust its way inside, piercing the sepulchral silence of the smoke-laden room, fogged over as completely as a sea-staring village on an early autumn morn. Another evening had come to an end at M—, gaming establishment.

Smythe, the establishment's aged servant and acknowledged sovereign of the wait staff, gave the casement window a shove and a brave gust of air raced inside. Alas, poor air. Although its origins were distinguished, coming as they did from the exalted breezes of the Atlantic, before being dropped upon the shore at Brighton — favorite pleasure ground of the Prince Regent and his spectacular circle of friends, admirers, and gapers — the sea air, fresh with the hope of morning, was no match for the stale air of the gaming room, weary with the memory of fortunes lost and hopes confounded the night before. Smythe, however, paid no heed to this atmospheric skirmish. Instead, like a general surveying a battlefield, confident of victory, he eagerly focused his still bright eye on the shambles that lay stretched out before him.

"Gentlemen, to work," he quietly commanded his small crew of assistants, and the hazy scene came to life. A regiment of empty bottles was regrouped onto waiting silver trays and transported out of the room, followed by a convoy of drained crystal goblets and crumb-splattered china plates. Battered playing cards, that lay scattered about the gaming tables like groaning soldiers left to die, were gathered up and returned to their casket-like wooden boxes. Overturned chairs, unceremoniously knocked about like dispossessed French aristocrats, were restored to their upright positions. Candle sconces, dripping with cascades of dried and yellowing wax, were shorn of their tallow tresses and polished until they gleamed anew.

"A bottle there, under the table," said Smythe, nodding in the direction of the far chandelier. Tom, the new boy and a lad of just thirteen, hurried to retrieve the straggler, but the bottle refused to abandon its position. He yanked on it again and discovered, to his surprise, Lord Lauferby, whose hand was firmly attached to the bottle's other end. While Tom hauled the young lord from out of his berth under the table, Smythe hurried over to help Lord Lauferby to his feet.

"Good morning, Milord," said Smythe as he straightened the young lord's soiled cravat. "Get Lord Lauferby's hat, Tom. You will probably find it under the table, as well. And check for anything else Lord Lauferby might have, ahem, stored there temporarily."

Tom dove under the table and retrieved the missing hat, but not before his quick eye noticed the young lord's purse lying nearby. He opened the clasp and glanced inside. His virtue was not tempted. Besides a crumpled IOU, a few small coins were the purse's only other occupants. Tom, who had bigger dreams, knew the filching of such a paltry sum was hardly worth the loss of his new job — and a possible subsequent appointment at the gallows.

"Here you are, Mister Smythe," said Tom, as he handed over the hat and the purse. "That one will be spending his evenings in debtors' prison before the year is out, wouldn't you say?"

"Nonsense. Impoverished lords do not go to prison," Smythe replied. They either marry the daughters of rich merchants or join the army and get themselves killed."

When Lord Lauferby was of a presentable enough appearance to greet the early morning streets of Brighton, Smythe led the tottering young man to the front door. "A little fresh air will do you a world of good, Milord. Here we are. Yes, that sun is bright. Watch the step. And the next one. Just one more, Milord. Excellent. Good-day, Milord. Mind the lamppost. Good-bye."

Lord Lauferby's feet, having found themselves upon firm ground, began to walk forward with a mind of their own — a good thing since the intellectual faculties housed within the lord's head were still too befuddled to take command — and the rest of his limbs followed their lead. Involuntarily, he raised his hat to a passing carriage, even though it was just the baker's assistant making his morning rounds. Then he instinctively bowed to a cheesemonger, an imposing figure with a stony countenance who glared at Milord as Lord Lauferby fell forward and nearly crashed through the cheese shop's plate glass window.

The cheesemonger remained at his post by the window until he was satisfied the young lord had gone on his way and the danger was past. He then removed a round of cheese from the carefully arranged window display and turned his attention to the young woman waiting at the counter.

Rosemary, kitchen maid to an establishment that rented rooms for the season, meals provided for an additional fee, gathered up her purchases, a thick wedge of aged cheese and a small pot of fresh butter, and left the shop. Her steps did not take her to the most fashionable section of town, nor did they take her to the quarter where the tradesmen lived. Instead, she hurried to a street that hovered on the margin of fashion, but only just. Walking sprightly past the main entrance of the house, where a small sign that said "Rooms to Let" was discreetly displayed in the bow window, she rounded the corner and flounced down a small flight of steps that led to the servants' entrance.

Inside the kitchen, the cook had removed the kettle from the fire and was filling a china teapot. The cook nodded to Rosemary as she entered, but mornings were not for chatting. Percy Ainsford Foster, the current Viscount Ashe and the house's most distinguished boarder, was most particular about taking his first breakfast at an early hour, one of the few wholesome habits he still retained from his early childhood. Rosemary therefore quickly opened her packages and cut off a generous slice of cheese. As she scooped out a spoonful of butter, the cook brought over two freshly baked rolls. While the cook gave the breakfast tray a final examination, Rosemary pinched her cheeks and adjusted her cap. Then she lifted up the tray and proceeded toward the stairs.

Lord Ashe's rooms were on the second landing, facing the back. Rosemary knocked on the door and waited for the familiar voice to answer. When no voice, familiar or otherwise, invited her to come inside, she knocked again.

"Milord?" she called out. "Milord?"

After checking that no one else was in the hall, she bent down and placed her eye next to the keyhole. She could see just enough to determine the curtains in the room were still drawn and that a figure, who was dressed in dinner clothes, had fallen asleep at the table. Thus reassured, she turned the handle of the door, which opened to her touch, and entered the room. After depositing the breakfast tray on a side table near the door, she walked over to the window and drew aside the curtain.

"Good morning, Milord," she said with a cheerful voice. "I hope his lordship is feeling quite well this morning. Shall I make a fire, before I set the table for breakfast? The room is rather chilly."

She waited for Lord Ashe to reply. However, the figure slumped over the table was silent. As she studied the back of the young man's head — she particularly liked the way his soft brown curls so carelessly swept the top of his shirt's stiffly upturned collar — a smile came to her lips. This would not be the first time he had played a trick on her. She therefore adjusted the bodice of her dress and gamely approached the table. When she was close enough to touch the brown curls with her outstretched hand, she said, softly, "Milord?"

It was only then, while she stood behind him, waiting, that she noticed that the uneasy chill that hung upon the air was not entirely of this world. Slowly, she circled round the table, until she stood in front of the young man, whose down-turned head rested upon his right arm, which rested, in turn, upon the table. His left arm, she observed, hung limply by his side.

"Milord?" she said again, as she reached out her hand and gently touched the fingers of Lord Ashe's right hand, which hung suspended over the table's edge, as though caught in flight and held there by some unseen force. Their coldness made her quickly take her hand away. And then she saw it — a small drop of liquid, red in color, like a tiny ruby pendant, that seemed to be attached to the under part of the young man's wrist.

The drop quivered and fell, and she followed its downward flight with mesmerized eyes. On the ground, under Lord Ashe's wrist, was a puddle, dark in color, but too thick to be wine. Rosemary looked at the liquid mass for several long seconds, puzzled. Then she slowly raised her eyes and, in the last moments before she collapsed onto the floor, screamed.

CANTO THE FIRST

C harlotte, dear, you must come down at once."

Lady Charlotte Ashe, who was standing at an open casement, sipping her morning chocolate as she took in the view of the gardens below, glanced over at her aunt, Mrs. Seymour.

"What is it, Auntie? Has a new fashion magazine from London arrived?"

"The constable is waiting for you, in the study."

"The constable?"

"I suggest you wear your grey muslin."

"Does he look as serious as all that?"

"He looks positively shattered. So do dress quickly."

Charlotte turned away, to conceal her wearily amused smile. She knew her aunt enjoyed nothing more than a juicy piece of gossip, a pleasure that was too often denied her at Hopewell, Charlotte's ancestral home, which stood in magnificent solitude in the mournfully silent Yorkshire countryside.

She also knew that Mrs. Seymour, who had been blessed with a cheerful and sociable disposition at birth, or so her aunt so often said, would never have willingly chosen to live so far from the chattering centers of society. However, Mrs. Seymour was a widow of reduced circumstances, and Charlotte was an orphan — a wealthy orphan, to be sure — and therefore bereft of parental guidance. When Charlotte's brilliant marriage to the dashing Lord Ashe was revealed to be an unfortunate mistake and she insisted upon a period of separation, Mrs. Seymour had dutifully answered the call of service. She had accompanied Charlotte to Hopewell, where she played the role of matronly chaperon to her young, attractive, and unprotected niece.

For these reasons and more Charlotte would not keep her aunt, who was surely longing to hear the constable's news, waiting in suspense longer than necessary. She returned her chocolate cup to the breakfast tray and said, "I shall dress as quickly as I can."

When Charlotte appeared in the study the constable, who was never entirely comfortable while in the presence of the gentry, nervously fingered the brim of his hat. Without raising his downcast eyes, he bobbed his head in her direction. Then he dispatched his commission with as much brevity as tact would allow.

Lord Ashe had been found dead in his rooms in Brighton. The family's solicitor, Mr. Inkerwell, who was already in Brighton, requested the immediate presence of Lady Ashe in that city. There were some matters that required her ladyship's urgent attention.

"Has Mr. Inkerwell gone mad? One does not jump in a carriage and go to Brighton. One needs clothes and — " Mrs. Seymour stopped in mid-sentence. She cast an anxious glance over at Charlotte, whose complexion had turned a worrisome shade of chalky white.

"I'm sure I don't know about Mr. Inkerwell's health, Ma'am," replied the constable, who raised his eyes from his hat for a moment to also steal a glance at the young woman. "But shall I reserve places on this afternoon's mail coach?"

"This afternoon? My niece could not possibly travel today. Not after having received such a shock."

"Yes, I can, Auntie." Charlotte turned to the constable and forced herself to smile. "Please do reserve the places for us. And thank you."

The constable fairly ran from the room, grateful for having discharged his duty and received his dismissal.

"But Charlotte … You look so pale. And what will you wear?"

"Tell Ella to get out the trunk with the mourning clothes I wore when Grandfather died. It has only been three years. Surely some of the dresses will still fit."

II.

The drawing room was of limited size and only passably elegant in its furnishings — it was always impossible to find suitable rooms to rent in the middle of the Brighton season — but the distinguished personage of Mr. Obadiah Inkerwell, solicitor, was enough to set the proper atmosphere for the solemn occasion. Grave in countenance and funeral in dress at even the happiest of occasions, he rose to even greater heights of sublime mournfulness when it was his unpleasant but necessary duty to break bad news to one of his clients. Since many of his clients belonged to the *ton*, the noble members of Regency society who were famous for getting themselves into embarrassing financial scrapes, it was a role he was accustomed to performing. Therefore, a certain nervous tapping of his right forefinger against his greying temple revealed an uneasiness that was totally unexpected.

Charlotte noticed the gesture but did not comment upon it. The journey to Brighton had been more exhausting than she had anticipated. The weather had been unseasonably hot, the coach had been uncomfortably stuffy, and the black mourning dress she was wearing ...

She glanced down at her hands. The ends of two black sleeves met her wrists. In her hands was a black satin fan. It was closed at the moment, but when it was open it revealed a suitably morbid scene of a patrician noblewoman dressed in elegant black crepe and draped over a marble tomb.

She supposed it would eventually become real to her: Her husband was dead; she was a widow. But for the moment it still seemed like an uncomfortable dream from which she would presently awake. This scene — with Mr. Inkerwell sitting in a gold and red striped chair, so unlike the sedate brown-upholstered chair in his solicitor's office — would fade into the gentle glow of a new morning at Hopewell. Instead of the sound of Mr. Inkerwell tapping his finger against his head, she would hear the tapping of her maid at her bedroom door. Her morning tray of chocolate would be placed by her bed. The curtains would be pulled aside and the windows opened. The fresh morning air would tumble into the room, bringing with it the joyful promise of a new day. If the weather promised to be fine she might spend the day sketching. And if not ...

"Shall I come directly to the point, Lady Ashe?" Mr. Inkerwell had stopped tapping his head.

Charlotte had her romantic side, which expressed itself in a love of all things beautiful, whether in nature or in art. But she had her practical side, as well. As she had no expectation of Mr. Inkerwell expressing himself in the heightened tones of poetic verse — he had been the family's solicitor since before she was born and so they knew one another very well — she replied, "Yes, please do."

"You are quite ruined."

Mrs. Seymour hiccupped. Still gasping for breath, she said, "Pray, Mr. Inkerwell, my niece has already received one great shock. Do spare her feelings and do not exaggerate what is already a most distressful situation."

"I assure you, Mrs. Seymour, I would not cause Lady Ashe unnecessary harm for the world. You are both well aware of Lord Ashe's passion for the gaming table."

"His sickness, I would say," interjected Mrs. Seymour with a look of pious indignation.

"How we express it, Ma'am, will not alter the situation. Lord Ashe's losses were immense. He gave vowels to many of his acquaintances ..."

"He gave what?" Mrs. Seymour asked, not sure if this was a suitable topic to be discussed in the presence of a young lady.

"Vowels, Ma'am. IOUs," explained Mr. Inkerwell. "And may you never have a need to form a closer acquaintance with those unfortunate pieces of paper. When a gentleman is unable to pay his gambling debts immediately, he hands his debtor a voucher, upon which is written a promise to pay his debt at a later date."

"But if these gentlemen are his friends, could they not forgive him and his debts?"

"I am afraid not, Mrs. Seymour. A gambling debt is a debt of honour, and honour is not a thing that can be foregone. There is also the matter of the money Lord Ashe owed to tradesmen in London, Brighton, Bath ..." His voice trailed off as he pointed to a thick stack of bills that rested upon the table.

"Shall I have to sell the sugar plantation in Jamaica?" Charlotte asked, trying to remain calm although her thoughts were racing with dizzying and distracting speed.

The plantation had belonged to her grandfather, who had gone to Jamaica as a young man to make his fortune. It was sugar that had enabled him to return to England a wealthy one. It was sugar that had enabled him to purchase a country home and an estate, Hopewell, that was worthy of a peer of the realm. And it was sugar that had enabled him to marry off his only surviving grandchild, Charlotte, to a gentleman — The Right Honorable The Viscount Ashe — who possessed the title that his own humble family lacked.

Having reviewed the history of the sugar plantation in her mind, Charlotte decided that if she must sell it to pay off her late husband's debts and clear his name she would willingly make the sacrifice. The plantation's profits had bought her material comforts, but they had not brought her happiness.

"The sugar plantation was sold in the winter."

The fan dropped from Charlotte's hands. A second hiccup burst from Mrs. Seymour's lips.

"But … The sugar plantation …" Mrs. Seymour blurt out, in between the hiccups, which were now coming fast and furious, "… He had no right!"

"He may have been wrong to do so, Mrs. Seymour, but I am afraid he did have the right." Mr. Inkerwell rose from his chair and picked up the dropped fan, which he placed in Charlotte's trembling hands. "You will recall, Lady Ashe, your grandfather was most insistent the marriage take place. He was very anxious that you marry into the nobility. Lord Ashe came from a distinguished family—"

"He did not have more than five thousand a year to live on," Mrs. Seymour muttered.

"Very true, Mrs. Seymour. Very true. This was not the first time an impoverished lord married the heiress to a large fortune made in trade. And it shall not be the last. But those were the facts. Your grandfather, Lady Ashe, settled everything upon your husband. I advised him not to do it. But your grandfather did want that title, both for you and for your ..."

"Yes, for my children." Charlotte opened the fan and looked down at the lady in mourning, who was weeping over her husband's tomb. There had not been any children. Perhaps if there had been children ... She snapped the fan shut. "So the plantation in Jamaica is gone?"

"Yes," Mr. Inkerwell replied with a voice filled with sorrow.

"Be brave, dear Charlotte, be brave," said Mrs. Seymour, having recovered somewhat from her initial shock. "We must bear the burden and accept the worst. This is no time to faint."

"I have no intention of fainting, Auntie." Charlotte then returned her gaze to Mr. Inkerwell. "I assume I cannot expect to receive income from my late husband's family estate at Ramblewood. When there is no heir, the estate goes to the nearest living male relation, does it not?"

Mr. Inkerwell slightly bowed his head to acknowledge her correct grasp of the English laws of inheritance.

"But even if there is no income from Ramblewood or from the plantation," Charlotte continued, "there are the rents from Hopewell. Surely, the income from the tenants' farms will be enough for us to live upon."

Mr. Inkerwell once again began to tap the side of his head.

"I assure you, my aunt and I live quite modestly."

Mr. Inkerwell continued to tap.

"Yorkshire is not London, or Brighton," Charlotte persisted. "Mr. Inkerwell, surely there will be enough for us to live quietly and respectably in my family's home. Surely my situation is not as bleak as you say."

"Hopewell is no longer yours, Lady Ashe. Your husband lost it in a bet."

Charlotte stared at Mr. Inkerwell.

"Even if he had not gambled away the last of your property, you must know you would most likely have lost your home. Suicide is a criminal offense in this country. The Crown has the right to confiscate the property of the deceased. That includes the property you brought to the marriage, as well as the Ashe family home at Ramblewood."

"Suicide?" Charlotte whispered, trying to make sense of what the solicitor had told her.

"I am sorry. I thought you knew. I left instructions for Dr. Thorpe to call upon you."

"It is impossible, Mr. Inkerwell," Mrs. Seymour cried out. "Think of the scandal!"

Although Charlotte did not wish to succumb to a fit of hysteria, like her aunt, for the first time in her life she really thought she might faint. If her husband was declared a suicide, he would not receive a proper burial. A stake would be thrust through his body, and the body would be unceremoniously tossed into a pit dug at some desolate and forsaken crossroads. It was true she had no love for the dead man. But she did have compassion for a fellow human being, and so she pleaded, "Can the doctor not find some other cause of death?"

"I am afraid not. The right wrist of Lord Ashe was slit with a pen knife, which was found lying on the floor beside the gentleman, in a pool of blood. If this was not a case of suicide, what else could it be? Murder?"

A loud thump made the solicitor start.

"Mrs. Seymour!" exclaimed Mr. Inkerwell, for that venerable lady had fainted and fallen onto the floor.

III.

Brighton is a pleasant place in the summer. The sea provides a picturesque background for the "my lords" and "my ladies" who stroll up and down the Steine, the small park favored by the Prince Regent. When that wholesome exercise becomes too taxing, refreshments can be had at any of the numerous shops whose sole purpose in the world is to serve that exalted class known as the English aristocracy. Should even taking a glass of lemonade prove to be too exhausting, there is always one pastime to occupy the hours that requires little exertion: gossiping about the latest scandal. For in Brighton there is always a latest scandal, although perhaps few are as exciting as the death of a viscount under unusual circumstances.

"Do not pay attention to them," advised Mrs. Seymour.

"To whom?" asked Charlotte, keeping her head erect and her gaze fixed firmly on the vista that lay before her.

Mrs. Seymour glanced over at a crush of pink and periwinkle blue parasols that carefully hid the faces of their owners, but not the peals of laughter. She then looked at her niece, shrouded in her black dress. The color of mourning was jarring in a place devoted to youth and beauty and pleasure — and conspicuous. Of course, there was nothing Charlotte could do. She was a widow. She must be dressed in black. Yet the cheeks of Mrs. Seymour burned crimson, out of sympathy for her niece, who had to publicly bear the shame of suicide, gambling debts, and who knew what else upon her slender shoulders.

"We turn in here, do we not?" asked Charlotte, when they reached the home of Mrs. Howe, a girlhood friend of Mrs. Seymour who had married off her only daughter to the son of a wealthy baronet who valued his comforts too much to gamble them away. Mrs. Howe had generously offered to play hostess to her old friend and the young widow — and had made sure all Brighton knew it.

"Yes, dear," replied Mrs. Seymour, giving the bell a tug. "You must not feel obligated to take tea with Mrs. Howe if you do not feel up to it. I shall make your excuses for you."

A servant opened the front door and bowed the two ladies inside. Charlotte was tempted to run up the stairs and collapse upon the bed. Although she had pretended not to notice the sniggers and the stares outside, each step from Mr. Inkerwell's rooms to the residence where they were staying had been a torture. But she could hear voices in the drawing room. It would be impolite not to at least pay her respects to her hostess. Furthermore, any display of weakness would be gossiped about later by the ladies, whose animated voices had drifted into the hallway.

Their conversation came to an abrupt halt when Charlotte and Mrs. Seymour appeared at the doorway of the drawing room. Mrs. Howe rose at once from the divan where she had been holding court and hurried to escort her guests to comfortable seats in the middle of the room, where all the ladies could see them.

"Lady Ashe, how pale you look," said Mrs. Howe, with just a trace of satisfaction. "Let me pour you a cup of tea."

While Mrs. Howe busied herself with the teapot, her daughter lazily adjusted the bejeweled bracelets that adorned her plump wrists and drawled, "We are all shocked, Lady Ashe, so terribly shocked."

The other ladies, as if they were actresses in a play who had just heard their cue, all chimed in at once to express their shock upon hearing the news and their concern for the poor young widow, whom they assured had only to say the word and they were at her service, to perform whatever little service they could. When Charlotte refused to either burst into tears or reveal details about her husband's suicide, the ladies lost interest. The conversation turned, instead, to the other burning issue of the day: the shocking exploits of Lord Byron. The first Cantos of *Childe Harold's Pilgrimage* had burst upon the scene just a few months earlier and immediately turned the poet into one of the most celebrated — and gossiped about — men in English society.

Only one lady remained silent, a patrician-looking woman who had entered the silver-haired years. She sat with her quizzing glass held up to her eye, unabashedly staring at Charlotte.

"I hear Lord March is in Brighton," said Mrs. Howe to the silver-haired woman, after she had handed the cups of tea to Charlotte and Mrs. Seymour.

The Dowager Countess of March lowered her eye piece. "Yes, he is."

"How comforting it must be to have your son close by you during this trying time. Your family is related to the Ashe family, is it not?"

"Lord March and the sixth Viscount of Ashe were second cousins." Lady March then turned her attention back to Charlotte and said, "You would not know my son, as he was not among Viscount Ashe's circle of friends."

"But your estates do adjoin one another, in Yorkshire, do they not, Lady March?" asked Mrs. Howe. "Is not your beautiful home at Lundsmoor Park adjacent to Ramblewood?"

Lady March kept her gaze fixed upon Charlotte while Mrs. Howe's daughter removed her attention from her baubles long enough to exclaim, "How fortunate for your family! If Lord March is the heir, the two estates will now be one!"

IV.

The next morning Charlotte was awakened by the sounds of Brighton beginning a new day. A tradesman's wagon rumbled down the cobblestone street. A dairyman called out his wares. Somewhere a bell jangled and a horse neighed to an acquaintance.

Charlotte went to the window, which faced the street, and pushed aside the curtain. A stream of sunshine rushed inside. It looked to be another perfect day. Under other circumstances she would have welcomed the chance to rent a bathing machine and go for a refreshing swim in the sea. Instead, she let the curtain fall back into place and forced herself to be content with splashing cold water onto her face.

The hour was still early and she wondered how she could fill it. She had no letters to write, since she did not have a wide circle of friends. She had grown up happy but secluded on her grandfather's estate. The friends she might have made as a new bride did not materialize. Her husband's circle tended to fritter away their earthly existence with eating and drinking and gambling. Since Charlotte had very little interest in any of those things, she had remained as socially isolated in London and Bath and Brighton as she had been, before her marriage, in Yorkshire.

If Charlotte had been at Hopewell, she could have filled the time before breakfast by taking a walk. But in Brighton it would not be proper to go for a walk unless she was accompanied by Mrs. Seymour, and Charlotte did not have the heart to rouse her companion, who was most likely exhausted by the long journey they had made the day before. Charlotte therefore reached for her copy of poems by William Wordsworth, which she had brought with her, and read:

> I wandered lonely as a Cloud
> That floats on high o'er Vales and Hills,
> When all at once I saw a crowd
> A host of dancing Daffodils;
> Along the Lake, beneath the trees,
> Ten thousand dancing in the breeze.

It was one of her favorite poems, but on this morning the lines of verse failed to engage her unsettled thoughts. She might feel lonely as a cloud, like the poet, but she could not dance with the daffodils, even if there were one hundred thousand of them dancing before her eyes.

Setting the book aside, she paced up and down the small room. A plan began to form in her mind. This plan was perhaps morbid, and more than a bit foolish, but the longer she thought about it the surer she became this was something she must do. And so she rang for her maid, Ella, who was sure to be up and about since Charlotte was convinced the sprightly young woman never slept more than a few hours. Indeed, Ella answered her lady's call within minutes, as though she had been waiting for the ring, bringing with her a tray crowned with a silver pot filled with steaming hot chocolate that had just been freshly made.

"Ella, do you think a carriage could be hired at this hour?" asked Charlotte.

"Yes, my lady," the maid replied, setting down the tray on a table, before going to the cupboard to remove Charlotte's black walking costume.

Charlotte smiled as she watched the maid's quick movements. Ella was invaluable. Not only was Ella efficient, but she was also endowed with a surfeit of youthful confidence. She had yet to meet the task that could confound her, and perhaps she would always be one of those women who were supremely confident and capable. For her sake, Charlotte hoped so. The person who could meet with failure and disappointment and not become crushed or embittered by the experience had a distinct advantage in life.

"Shall we be returning to Hopewell?" Ella asked, as she removed a miniscule spot of dirt that clung to the hem of the long black pelisse, a souvenir from the dusty mail coach that had brought them to the seaside resort.

"No, I wish to go somewhere else, somewhere here, in Brighton. And I would like you to come with me."

Ella gave her mistress a quick quizzical look, but did not say a word. That was another thing Charlotte valued in Ella. The maid, though young in years, did not jabber. She knew how to keep her thoughts — and other's secrets — to herself.

"Yes, my lady. Shall I take out the bonnet with the veil?"

When the carriage came to a stop it was in front of a nondescript building that had a "Rooms to Let" sign sitting in its front window. As Charlotte studied the building's slightly frayed facade, a sense of dread dulled her sense of purpose. It was inside that building that her husband had lived his final days. It was there he had spent his last moments.

There was no reason for her to visit the scene. Mr. Inkerwell had come to Brighton for the express purpose of taking care of the arrangements, so she would be spared from all unpleasantness. He could be relied upon to perform the task with tact and efficiency. Her presence in Brighton was needed only to give her approval and sign some papers. So why had she come to this place? What gloomy cloud was leading her onward? Was it only a need to say goodbye, something her husband had cheated her of, just as he had cheated her of domestic happiness while he was still alive? Or was it something else?

"My lady?" Ella asked, glancing pensively at her mistress's face.

Charlotte roused herself from her thoughts. She saw that the coachman was standing on the pavement, holding open the door to the carriage, anxious to be on his way. She stepped down from the carriage and deposited a few coins into his hand. She had an impulse to say, "You did not see me. You drove no one to this house this morning." But she did not. Why should she be afraid? What crime had she committed that she needed to conceal her actions?

Ella had already gone up the steps and struck up an acquaintance with the worn brass knocker that graced the front door. When the door opened, Ella handed the servant one of Charlotte's visiting cards. The servant went slightly pale when she saw the name, but she held the door open and gave an awkward curtsy as Charlotte glided inside.

Charlotte was shown into the front sitting room. Ella was also allowed to enter, at Charlotte's request. A few moments later Mrs. Barker, the establishment's proprietor, entered the room and introduced herself. After expressing a few words of sympathy, appropriate to her station, she waited for Charlotte to reveal the reason for this early morning visit.

"Is any money owed you for Lord Ashe's lodgings?"

"Mr. Inkerwell has taken care of everything, my lady."

Charlotte knew the solicitor had done so, but it was a way to begin. She only needed the strength to continue.

"Might I see ... the room ..."

Mrs. Barker, herself dressed in widow's clothes, stared at the youthful black-clad apparition standing before her. Years of being a widow with only moderate means had hardened the expression in her eyes. And so if she felt pity for the fresh recruit to the widows' ranks, she did not show it.

"I know Mr. Inkerwell will arrange for the removal of Lord Ashe's things, if he has not already done so," Charlotte continued, mustering up her confidence. "But I would like to see the room where ... it happened."

"There has never been a scandal in my house before," replied Mrs. Barker, who remained standing so her body blocked the entrance to the hallway.

Did the woman want more money, Charlotte wondered? No, she decided, the hard look in the landlady's eye did not come from greed.

Charlotte glanced around the sitting room. There was not much furniture, but what was there was clean and freshly polished. It was a perfectly respectable room, and Charlotte realized it most likely had not been easy for someone like Mrs. Barker to maintain that level of respectability, if she were alone in the world. The line that separated the genteel poor from the social outcast was thin, and in a place like Brighton it could be easily blurred before one knew what had happened. The landlady could therefore probably forgive an impoverished lord who escaped from her premises in the middle of the night with his bill unpaid. But suicide was a different matter. It would leave an indelible stain of notoriety upon the reputation of the woman's house. It would be remarked upon, by curious passersby, who would say, as they pointed to the second floor, "That is where it is happened. That is where Lord Ashe took his life."

She wished her husband had thought about that — thought about the effect his actions would have on others. If he was set on doing the deed, he had a whole sea to drown himself in. The sea would survive the shame. And at least there would have been the possibility of calling his death an accident. But despite his perfect manners, her husband had lacked any true feelings of consideration for others. She had discovered that, after it was too late.

"I am sorry," Charlotte murmured softly.

Mrs. Barker stepped aside.

V.

"Ella, please open the curtains."

A young servant girl, Rosemary, had shown them up to the second floor and led them to the door, but had refused to go inside. Charlotte did not press the matter. She had Ella to rely on, and Ella did not disappoint her. But even with the curtains drawn aside and the casement window thrown open, the room clung to its air of damp and gloom, as back rooms so often did. It was not that the room was dingy, or shabby. Charlotte's initial impression of Mrs. Barker's establishment had been correct. Through the door that led to the small bedroom, she could see the bed linens had been recently laundered and pressed. In the sitting room, where they stood, the upholstered furniture was not luxurious, but it was not threadbare either. What the room did lack, though, was sunlight and fresh air. However, Charlotte assumed her husband probably had not spent much time in the room, and so he would not have minded.

"Shall I open the cupboard, my lady?"

"Yes, please do."

They were both still standing by the window, avoiding the table that stood in the center of the room, and the dark spot that stained the wood floor.

"Perhaps my lord left behind a letter," said Ella, as she went over to the cupboard.

"Yes, perhaps he did," replied Charlotte, grateful to have a respectable reason for her being there. "Ella, would you mind looking through the clothes?"

Ella did not mind, but when she opened the door to the cupboard she gave a little gasp. Lord Ashe's clothes lay in a jumbled heap at the bottom of the cupboard.

"Someone has been here before us, and that someone is none too tidy," she said, with more than a hint of disapproval.

"Check the pockets anyway," said Charlotte. "If one of Mrs. Barker's servants was looking for money, they might have left a letter untouched."

Ella went to work. Because the jumble offended the maid's sense of order, she began to hang the coats and waistcoats upon their pegs, after she had made a search through their pockets.

Charlotte was glad Ella had accepted her explanation that an unscrupulous servant must have entered the room and searched for any valuables that had been left behind. She, however, was not so easily convinced. Would a servant, who was sure to be the first one suspected if something valuable was missing, be so careless? Would he willingly draw attention to the fact that the dead man's belongings had been rifled through?

Yet who else could have entered the room? The doctor would not have concerned himself with her husband's belongings. Mr. Inkerwell might have directed his assistants to go through the things, but he never would have allowed those assistants to behave in such a disrespectful manner. It was also unlikely behavior for the constable and his men.

That her husband would have been so careless with his clothes was unthinkable. A gentleman might not have a shilling in his waistcoat's pocket, but the waistcoat would be spotless and freshly pressed. So who had been in the room?

She turned and looked to see if the room showed other signs of disturbance. There was not much furniture to examine. Still avoiding the table that sat in the center of the room, she went over to a sofa positioned against a wall. Rounded pillows sat at either end. She slipped her hand underneath one of them. Nothing had been hidden there. There was nothing underneath the other pillow either, and she was beginning to feel foolish for looking. If her husband had written a letter to her, it was unlikely he would have hidden it. But was that why she had come? Was that what she was looking for?

She knew, in her heart, there was no letter. What could her husband have written?

Sorry, my love, for selling your estates to pay my debts. Fondly, Ashe

But if it was not a letter, what was she looking for?

"You are shivering, my lady. Shall I shut the window?"

"No, I want the air. Ella, perhaps we should not have tidied up the clothes. Just look through the pockets and leave the rest as they were."

"Yes, my lady," Ella replied, though she was not happy.

Charlotte took a deep breath and walked over to the table that stood in the middle of the room. She now knew what she was looking for — some clue that would explain why someone had wanted to murder her husband. And despite the opinion of Dr. Thorpe and Mr. Inkerwell, it had to have been murder. Her husband had loved life too much to have willingly parted from it of his own accord. Even though he had been forced to rent rooms in an unfashionable residence, his innate sense of optimism — "sense of optimism" were his words, she had called it a lack of seriousness — would have prevented him from succumbing to despair. True, wagering Hopewell at the gaming table could be construed as an act of desperation. But Charlotte knew her husband and his circle too well. It was very possible Lord Ashe had simply been drunk.

"Don't think about Hopewell. Not now," she whispered under her breath. She would have ample time to do that after she returned to Yorkshire. Today she had work to do. She had to clear her husband's name and restore his reputation. And now that she no longer felt like a thief rummaging through her estranged husband's belongings, trying to steal secrets he most likely wanted to hide, she felt up to the task.

The table did not look like it had been disturbed. Her husband's writing box, a large and bulky affair, sat in a prominent place. The box contained several sheaves of paper, as well as a supply of quill pens. A bottle of ink, uncapped, sat on the table. Beside it was a pen that had been only briefly used, since its tip was still sharp to the touch.

Her husband must have been in the process of writing a letter at the time he was murdered, Charlotte decided. The murderer then removed both the letter and the blotting paper, since both were missing. It was unfortunate the murderer had been so thorough. If he had left behind even a portion of the blotting paper, he would have left behind an important clue.

What was in that letter, she wondered? And who was it for? Was her husband trying to warn someone of an impending danger? Was that why he was murdered? Because he knew too much?

Charlotte smiled grimly. Her imagination was running away with her, as it often did. Her Aunt Seymour often playfully suggested that Charlotte should use her talents to write novels, as so many ladies of the era did. Perhaps she would do that, now that she had no money. But if her imagination was inventing stories about a letter that might not even exist, the jumbled clothes were real. So were the opened bottle of ink and the freshly sharpened quill pen. Someone had searched through the clothes. Someone had removed the letter, or at least prevented her husband from writing one.

Until then she had avoided going over to the side of the table where the pool of blood had stained the floor. Now she forced herself to do so. She tried to imagine her husband during his last moments, while seated at the table, not to be macabre, but to see it as the murderer must have seen it, before he removed the letter and the blotting paper and stole away. But something was bothering her. Something did not seem quite right.

"I've finished with the clothes, my lady."

Charlotte gave a start. She had not heard Ella approach her.

"Oh, look! There's your grandfather's snuff box." Ella reached for a silver box that was sitting on the table, behind the bottle of ink, and handed it to her mistress. "Surely no one will mind if you keep it, my lady. It does still belong to you, even if you gave it to Lord Ashe as a gift."

Charlotte looked down at the heavy silver box. It was not the sort of snuff box gentlemen carried with them, since it was much too large. Instead, her grandfather had used it to store the specially-blended snuff mixture he ordered from a shop in London. After her grandfather passed away, she had given the box to her husband, even though it was dear to her because of its sentimental value.

At least he had not sold the box or pawned it, Charlotte thought with relief, as she opened the heavy silver lid. She was not totally surprised to discover the box was empty. Her husband had had many faults, but an addiction to snuff was not one of them. So why had he kept the box, when he could have sold it to pay off a gambling debt?

"Ella, please do close the window. I am feeling a little chilled."

That was not entirely true. But she wanted to be alone with the box for a minute, unobserved. The box had a secret compartment, which was revealed by activating a hidden spring. She pressed hard on the place and the false bottom sprung upward. Lying at the bottom of the box was a small silver locket.

She placed the box back on the table and removed the locket with trembling fingers. It was not one of hers. She knew by the engraved design that graced the locket's cover. A part of her did not wish to discover what was inside the locket. A part of her wished she had never come to this hateful room filled with so many secrets and lies. But she had come, and so she forced herself to open the locket and see what was inside.

A lock of hair, black as a midnight sky, nestled inside its silver bed. Charlotte's hair was light brown in color. A sickening feeling stole over her as she stared at the lock of hair. Was that it? she wondered. Had her husband been murdered because of some sordid love affair?

"What are you doing here?"

Charlotte snapped the locket shut and slipped it into her reticule, before she turned toward the door, to discover who had spoken.

A gentleman, who looked to be in his mid-thirties and of high rank, if his imperious manner was any indication, stood in the doorway, glowering. However, when Charlotte turned, and he realized the woman in black was also a person of rank, he softened his tone of voice.

"Lady Ashe?"

"Yes."

"I beg your pardon. The servant did not say it was you who was in this room. I am Lord March. I believe my mother, Lady March, had the pleasure of making your acquaintance yesterday."

"Yes, we did meet. Lady March reminded me we have a family connection."

"That is why I am here. You have not disturbed anything in the room, I hope?"

Charlotte stole a guilty glance over at the cupboard. Ella had already made a hasty retreat behind her mistress.

Lord March strode over to the cupboard, whose contents were much neater than they had been a few minutes earlier, and demanded, "Why did you tidy up the clothes?"

"Why do you care?" Charlotte replied, angry at being treated like a child caught sneaking a fruit pie from the pantry. "They are my husband's things, not yours."

Lord March colored slightly at the reprimand. It was evident he was not accustomed to being spoken to in such a manner. But he did not lash back, as he might have done to someone else. Instead, he closed the cupboard door and said, "It *was* evidence."

"Of what?" Charlotte knew the answer, but she was still too angry to admit she had done something foolish. If only she had slept late, or gone for a walk, or done anything rather than come to this detested place.

"Evidence that the room had been disturbed," Lord March was saying. "Evidence that perhaps your husband …"

"Was murdered? Do not be afraid to say the word. I understand murder is preferable to suicide. But one of Mrs. Barker's servants might have searched through the clothes. Surely the blotting paper is of more importance."

Lord March raised an eyebrow and studied her closely. Charlotte recalled the way Lady March had examined her, through the quizzing glass, and it struck her that perhaps there was more to the older woman's inquisitiveness than curiosity to see how a young woman suddenly widowed was bearing up under the strain.

"What blotting paper are you referring to, Lady Ashe, if I may ask?"

"The piece that is missing, of course."

Lord March walked over to the table and made a quick survey of the objects that sat upon it. "That was clever of you to notice," he said. "But perhaps Lord Ashe was disturbed before he had the opportunity to write his letter."

"Perhaps." Charlotte felt she could be gracious, now it had been established she was not a child.

"And how do you explain …" Lord March picked up the heavy silver snuff container, whose lid was still open and whose secret false bottom was plainly revealed. "… this."

Charlotte tried very hard not to turn crimson. She could easily explain the box. But she had no intention of speaking about the locket to a man she had met only a few minutes earlier, and who had no right to pry into her personal affairs. Fortunately, she did not have to speak, since the sound of loud footsteps on the stairs gave her a natural excuse to turn away.

Constable Brickwall entered, followed by two other men. One was his assistant, a sallow-complexioned young man who looked like he spent his time in the dark alleyways of London, instead of chasing criminals in the bracing Brighton air. The other man, Theo Bryght, was a Bow Street Runner from London. He had come to Brighton to enjoy the many pleasures the seaside resort had to offer. But since his chief pleasure was solving crimes he had readily foregone a swim in the sea to take a look at the scene of Lord Ashe's death.

Although Constable Brickwall, as the representative of the law in Brighton, should have been the one to take charge, he was happy to defer to the Runner from London. Constable Brickwall was not fond of criminals, who were often dangerous men. He therefore tended to stay in his rooms, where he played cards with his assistant and smoked his pipe with his friends, unless he absolutely had to become involved. He had inspected the room on the day Lord Ashe's body was found. But since the examining doctor had proclaimed the deceased was a suicide — a verdict Constable Brickwall was more than happy to accept — he had spent no more than a quarter of an hour at the scene of the crime. The constable would have ignored the summons to revisit the room if that summons had not come from Lord March, a peer of the realm.

And so after Constable Brickwall made the introductions, it was Theo Bryght who bowed stiffly in Charlotte's direction, scowled at Ella, and looked suspiciously at Lord March, before saying, "I thought this was to have been a private interview, Lord March. I presume all the fresh evidence has been trampled upon, tampered with, and otherwise disturbed during this morning *tete-a-tete.*"

"Constable Brickwall had his chance to examine the room when Lord Ashe's body was first discovered," Lord March replied coolly.

Mr. Bryght replied by ignoring Lord March and striding over to the open cupboard. "This is what you wished us to see, my lord?"

"Yes," replied Lord March. "The clothes were in order when I was here three days ago." Lord March then turned to Charlotte and said, "I am staying in Brighton. When I heard your family solicitor had arrived, I offered my assistance. I came with Mr. Inkerwell and Dr. Thorpe to see the ... room."

After staring for a few moments at what was left of the jumbled heap of clothes, Mr. Bryght turned to Lord March and asked, "And why did you come this morning?"

"Me?"

"You had a silver box in your hand when we entered the room. Were you looking for something, my lord?"

Charlotte noticed the silver box was back on the table. The lid was shut. Lord March must have quickly put the false bottom back in its place. She wondered why he had done so, instead of leaving the box open, but now was not the time to ask. The Bow Street Runner was not a fool, she realized. Whether that was fortunate or not was still to be determined.

If Lord March was disturbed by the Runner's keen observation, he did not show it. He answered the second question that had been put to him calmly, saying, "When you and the constable arrived, I was considering the fact that if an ordinary thief had entered the room he would not have left behind a silver box, which is perhaps the most valuable object in this entire establishment. Therefore, the person who was here last night must have been the murderer of Lord Ashe. He must have remembered that an incriminating piece of evidence had been left behind and come looking for it."

"How do you know this person was here last night? Perhaps it was the night before. Or yesterday afternoon. Or this morning."

"You are correct, Mr. Bryght. I spoke hastily when I made an assumption about the hour."

"Could it also be possible you spoke hastily when you assumed the person who entered this room was a murderer? Might it not be possible he is a friend of the family, who came here and left the clothes in disarray on purpose, to have it look like Lord Ashe did not commit suicide?"

"I did not touch Lord Ashe's clothes," Lord March replied. "I came here this morning at the invitation of the family, as I informed Constable Brickwall in my message. They asked me to oversee the packing up of Lord Ashe's things."

"They? Who are they?"

"Lord and Lady Cunningham. Lady Cunningham is the sister of the deceased."

"So Lord March was not acting in accordance with your instructions, my lady?" Mr. Bryght asked, shifting his piercing gaze to Charlotte.

"No," she replied.

Theo Bryght kept his gaze fixed upon Charlotte. This was worse than being accused of stealing a fruit pie from the pantry, she decided. This was like being accused of stealing the silver.

"And you, Lady Ashe? Why are you here?"

Charlotte decided to tell the same story she had told herself. True, it had not convinced her, but she did not know what else to say. Her power of imagination had deserted her at the moment when she needed it the most. "I wished to see the place where Lord Ashe died. Is that so strange?"

"I understand it was not a happy marriage."

"That is true," said Charlotte. "But we were man and wife. I thought perhaps Lord Ashe had left behind a letter for me, something that would explain ..."

Charlotte allowed her words to trail off as she raised her handkerchief to her eyes, which were dry, but the Bow Street Runner did not have to know that. It was obvious the man thought she and Lord March were working together to change the verdict from suicide to murder. She had no idea if that was a crime. As she had no wish to find out, she decided she would play the part of the fragile-as-a-rosebud distraught widow if that was what was necessary to arouse the compassion of the London Runner.

"And did Lord Ashe leave behind a letter, my lady?" Mr. Bryght droned on.

"I do not know. I did not find one. But I did see that his pen and ink had been removed from his writing box —"

"And his knife, my lady," said Mr. Bryght, studying first Charlotte and then Lord March. "Do not forget that his pen knife had also been removed from the writing box — and placed here."

The Runner removed the pen knife from his pocket and placed it on the floor, near the table.

"Is this where you found it, Constable?"

Constable Brickwall, who in truth did not remember exactly where the pen knife had fallen, grunted and said, "Close enough."

"I have not forgotten the knife," said Lady Ashe. "Yet there is no letter, nor is there any blotting paper."

"Lord Ashe might have changed his mind," said the sallow-faced assistant. "He might have thought to write a letter and changed his mind and slit his wrist instead."

Theo Bryght, who had been staring down at the pen knife, turned to the assistant and gave a nod of appreciation. The assistant grinned, showing off, in the process, two rows of yellow, tobacco-stained teeth.

"Yes, Lord Ashe might have changed his mind," said Mr. Bryght, scooping up the knife and returning it to his pocket. He then turned his attention to the writing box, and after he had rummaged through it he added, "But Lady Ashe is correct. There is no blotting paper in this box. You missed that in your initial examination of the room, Constable Brickwall."

Constable Brickwall shrugged. "Perhaps Lord Ashe finished his supply and forgot to order more."

"Or didn't have money to buy more," said the assistant, still grinning.

"Perhaps," said Mr. Bryght. "There could be any number of reasons why there is no blotting paper in this writing box. But this box ..."

Mr. Bryght picked up the silver snuff box. It took him only a few seconds to discover the mechanism that unlocked the false bottom. After gazing at the empty space for several long moments, he looked up at Lord March and said, "There was something in the bottom of this box three days ago."

"The box was empty when I looked inside it this morning," Lord March said slowly and with deliberation. "You may search me, if you do not wish to accept my word."

"I would not dream of doubting your word, my lord," said Mr. Bryght, who generally knew, from experience, when a person was lying and when a person was telling the truth.

The Bow Street Runner turned his attention back to Charlotte. She noticed that the man had the most brilliant blue eyes she had ever seen. But they weren't blue like the soft glow of a cloudless sky on a summer day. Instead, they glinted like sapphires—hard, cold, and compelling. As though mesmerized by those eyes, Charlotte felt herself, against her will, begin to extend the hand that held her reticule. But before she could do so, the London man abruptly turned away.

"There is a perfectly straightforward reason why a certain person might wish to remove something from this box," said Mr. Bryght, putting the silver box back on the table. "But that does not mean this person is the only one who was looking for the object that was in it."

Mr. Bryght walked over to his colleague. "The death of Lord Ashe becomes interesting, does it not, Constable?"

"Does it?" replied Constable Brickwall, looking not at all happy.

"If I am not mistaken there are secrets hidden in this room, and one of them is murder."

VI.

Although nothing had yet been proved, the Bow Street Runner's opinion that Viscount Ashe had been murdered was enough to save the young lord's body from the ignominy of a disgraceful burial. Mr. Inkerwell, assisted by Lord March, arranged for the coffin to be discretely transported to Ramblewood, the family's country estate in Yorkshire, where the last Viscount Ashe would receive a quiet burial in the graveyard of the parish church that was nearby.

All that was expected of Charlotte was to make her way to Yorkshire, in a separate carriage. Since Ella was more than capable of packing up the things of Charlotte and Mrs. Seymour, there was very little for Charlotte to do during her last day in Brighton. Mrs. Seymour had suggested a stroll along the seaside promenade, but Charlotte was in no mood for healing sunshine and invigorating air. The locket had been the final blow. Gambling debts she might have been able to pardon, with time. But the lock of hair was surely proof her husband had been enamored of another woman. If he had sold Hopewell to buy that woman's affections, she was sure she would never be able to find it in her heart to forgive him, and she did not wish to be persuaded to be charitable.

Having nothing to do, and not caring, for she was content to remain in a brown study, Charlotte sat in the library, a room Mrs. Howe and her daughter were more than happy to lend for her use, as they had no use for it themselves. The baronet, who might be expected to entertain his gentlemen friends in the library, was out.

Although a book lay open on the side table, Charlotte's attention was fixed, instead, upon the silver locket, which she perversely carried with her wherever she went. The locket was an ordinary affair. Its front was engraved with a floral design that swirled about the gleaming surface but signified nothing. It was the sort of thing one might purchase at a Cheapside jeweler's establishment, or even a Brighton dealer's pawn shop. Her husband's lover must have been terribly hard up for money, if she bought her trinkets in places like that. And if a woman with no fortune could engage her husband's heart, while she with her fifty thousand pounds could not … well, that was yet another sting.

When Charlotte had finished examining the outside of the locket for possibly the hundredth time, she opened it and stared — again, possibly for the hundredth time — at the letters that were engraved into the inside of the cover: *Psalm Ten, Verse Two*. She had not had the courage to search out the meaning of the inscription the night before, when she studied the locket by the romantic glow of candlelight. In such a light words engraved on a locket too strongly suggested the language of love letters, secret murmurings that were not meant to be casually read by an outsider's eye. For the lover, each phrase would be filled with momentous meaning. Even a dash or comma might be puzzled over until it was discovered to contain an entire world. Or so she supposed. Lord Ashe had been her first and only suitor. There had been no extended absence in between their meeting and their marriage, and so she had not received any letters from him worth keeping and cherishing.

"Psalm Ten, Verse Two," she slowly read aloud. In the morning sunlight those words sounded less … less what, she wondered? If her husband had loved the lady with the black hair, that love had ended with his death. Perhaps the lady was dead, too. If this love was no longer a living thing, the words could not hurt her, too much.

She went over to the bookcase and after a few minutes search she found a Bible. She turned the pages until she arrived at the *Book of Psalms* and the psalm that was tenth in number. With her finger she followed the words of the second verse:

The wicked in his pride doth persecute the poor: let them be taken in the devices that they have imagined.

That was an odd verse for lovers to choose, she thought. She examined the locket again, thinking that perhaps she had misread the inscription. But the letters were very clear: *Psalm Ten, Verse Two.*

"Another mystery," she said with a sigh, closing the book.

While she returned the Bible to its place on the shelf, she heard the sound of heavy boots approaching the room. A servant entered and announced that Mr. Theo Bryght wished to see her.

"Show him in," Charlotte replied, quickly wrapping the locket inside a handkerchief and then shoving the black cloth up her sleeve, with only a moment to spare before the man entered.

"You did not sleep well, Lady Ashe?" said the Bow Street Runner, immediately noting the slight traces of purple under Charlotte's tired eyes.

"Apparently the Brighton air does not agree with me."

"Perhaps something is worrying you?"

"Would that be unusual for a woman in my situation?"

"No. Losing one's husband and all one's money would keep most people awake at night. And I see you have turned to the Bible for solace. That is a very admirable thing to do."

Charlotte glanced over at the bookcase. In her haste she had not properly aligned the Bible with its neighbors, and so the book's spine was jutting slightly ahead of the others. Once again she was forced to admire the Runner's perceptive eye.

Mr. Bryght removed the Bible from the shelf and slowly turned the book's pages. Keeping his eyes turned downward, he commented, "It will be quicker, Lady Ashe, if you tell me what you found in the snuff box."

"What makes you think I found anything?"

"I do not claim to be a prophet, but I have been a Bow Street Runner for many years. A Runner, if he is any good at his work, learns to recognize the smell of danger."

"You believe I am dangerous?"

"I do not believe you murdered your husband, if that is what is stopping you from confiding in me. Yet I am not entirely convinced that a young woman so recently widowed would have the presence of mind to notice a piece of blotting paper, especially one that was not there. Perhaps Lord Ashe did leave behind a letter, before he took his life, and placed it in the snuff box—"

"No!"

Charlotte bit her lip, in an attempt to prevent herself from blurting out more. When she felt sufficiently in control of her emotions, she added, "There was no letter in the snuff box, Mr. Bryght."

"But there was something hidden in it, was there not?"

When Charlotte did not reply, he continued, saying, "Lady Ashe, if your husband was murdered it is possible the murderer returned to the room to retrieve an incriminating object. Should the murderer discover this object is now in your possession, you could be in great danger."

When Charlotte was still silent, he said, "Of course, if the murderer was Lord March, I can understand your reticence."

"Lord March?"

"Especially if it were more convenient, for the two of you, that Lord Ashe should receive his eternal reward at an earlier age than his natural good health might warrant."

"What exactly are you suggesting, Mr. Bryght?"

"I am suggesting, Lady Ashe, that you are a liar, an adulteress, and a murderer. Mind you, I personally do not believe any of those things, and I really do wish you would have told me what was in that snuff box before I was reduced to such reprehensible behavior. But I am in your power, and if you do not tell me what I wish to know I shall be forced to stoop even lower and add to the list that you drink, pull the tails of cats, and are, Ma'am, a Luddite."

Charlotte burst out laughing. It was a relief to feel that the tension between them had been dispelled. Yet even though she wanted to speak she could not. She could feel the locket pressing against her wrist, branding her heart with another sharp burst of hot shame. She therefore said, "I understand your need to examine this matter thoroughly, Mr. Bryght, but I cannot help but feel you are giving undo importance to this box."

Mr. Bryght bowed and resumed his study of the Bible, carefully turning the pages one by one. He was usually not so patient a man. In other circumstances, he would have left his card and tried his luck on another day. But he remained for two reasons. He enjoyed being in the presence of Lady Ashe, and his instincts told him she really might be in danger.

"Ah, here it is," he said, removing a strand of light-brown hair. "My mother also used to read the *Book of*

Psalms when her heart was troubled, may her soul rest in peace. But I do not recall the tenth psalm being one of her favorites."

Mr. Bryght lifted the book and began to read:

Why standest thou afar off, O Lord? Why hidest thou thyself in times of trouble? The wicked in his pride doth persecute the poor: let them be taken in the devices that they have imagined. For the wicked boasteth of his heart's desire, and blesseth the covetous, whom the Lord abhorreth. The wicked, through the pride of his countenance, will not seek after God: God is not in all his thoughts. His ways are always grievous; thy judgments are far above out of his sight: as for all his enemies, he puffeth at them. He hath said in his heart, I shall not be moved: for I shall never be in adversity. His mouth is full of cursing and deceit and fraud: under his tongue is mischief and vanity. He sitteth in the lurking places of the villages: in the secret places doth he murder the innocent: his eyes are privily set against the poor.

Mr. Bryght paused and looked up at Charlotte. "An interesting psalm. Your grandfather made his fortune in Jamaica, did he not?"

"Yes, he owned a sugar plantation," Charlotte replied without hesitation, feeling herself to be on safe ground.

"Did he have any enemies? Did you ever hear stories of workers that he mistreated?"

"I cannot believe my grandfather ever mistreated anyone. He came from humble beginnings, himself. He knew what it was to be poor."

"Was Lord Ashe involved in the management of the plantation, after your marriage? Might he have instituted practices considered to be objectionable by some of the plantation's laborers?"

"Lord Ashe was not interested in business matters. An overseer was in charge of the plantation, Mr. Tyson. He has been a trusted employee of my grandfather since before I was born."

Mr. Bryght returned his attention to the Bible and silently read a few more of the psalm's verses. Then he said, "Here is something interesting. Listen. 'Break thou the arm of the wicked and the evil man.' Our poor psalmist is asking for revenge. True, a slit wrist is not the same as a broken arm, but perhaps I was wrong about you, after all."

"What?" Charlotte hated the way this man always caught her off guard.

"Did you not say your family was once poor? Are you not poor now? Surely more than once you must have cursed the day you fell under the spell of a wastrel whose tongue was filled with 'mischief and vanity'."

"You are speaking of my late husband, Mr. Bryght, and a peer of the realm."

"My apologies, Ma'am," he replied, bowing slightly. "But I am puzzled, and I am not ashamed to admit it. Surely there are other psalms that would have brought more solace to a lady in your situation. So if you have no complaints against the wicked, why were you reading this particular psalm?"

Once again Charlotte could feel the Runner's cold blue eyes boring through her. It would be better to have this man on her side than continually against her, she decided. Besides, she was sure a man with so much persistence would eventually discover the existence of her late husband's mistress, without her help. She therefore removed the handkerchief from her sleeve, undid its folds, and handed the locket to the Runner.

"*Psalm Ten, Verse Two*," he read aloud. "Well, that explains your choice of reading matter, my lady." He then referred back to the Bible and read, "'The wicked in his pride doth persecute the poor: let them be taken in the devices that they have imagined.' Yes, a most interesting psalm."

"Mr. Bryght, could it be that Lord Ashe borrowed a large sum of money from a tradesman and neglected to pay it back? I have heard of instances where men have become impoverished due to their misplaced faith in the promises made by the nobility. Could someone like that have murdered my husband?"

"At this early stage in the investigation, anything is possible. But your theory does not address the question of the lock of hair."

"Does yours?"

"I have no theory, Lady Ashe, not yet. To construct a theory, one must choose a path, and to choose one path means not choosing another. At this point I wish to travel freely, wherever my nose leads me. And I beg your pardon for asking, my lady, but did Lord Ashe have a mistress?"

Charlotte was ready for the question. "I do not know," she said. "Lord Ashe and I lived in separate residences."

"That is why Lady Cunningham is making the funeral arrangements?"

"Yes, I suppose so."

"And who is Lord March to you, or Lady Cunningham?"

"I do not understand the question."

"Would it not have been more natural for Lord Cunningham to come to Brighton and make the necessary arrangements?"

"Lord and Lady Cunningham live in Yorkshire."

"You also live in Yorkshire, my lady, and yet you came."

"I was Lord Ashe's wife. And I believe Lord March said he was already in Brighton."

"In a matter so sensitive, would not one wish to involve just the family?"

"Lord March is related to the family. He was my late husband's second cousin."

Mr. Bryght's eyes narrowed until only two tiny specks of blue showed. "Where does he stand in terms of the inheritance?"

"I do not know."

"I suggest you find out, my lady."

"Mr. Bryght, surely you cannot believe Lord March had anything to do with my husband's murder. He is a —"

"Peer of the realm. Yes, Lady Ashe, I am aware of that fact. But do you find nothing strange about Lord March's eagerness to become involved in such a distasteful matter, or his returning to the room so early yesterday morning?"

"I assumed Lord March only wished to be helpful."

"And what about Mr. John Collins? Was he also only being helpful?"

"Who?"

"You are not familiar with the name?"

"No."

"Mr. Collins is the new owner of Hopewell."

"Oh." Charlotte could not say more.

VII.

Ramblewood, as its name suggested, had its beginnings as an impossibly drafty castle that was situated in the midst of a rambling forest. Some said it dated back to the time of The Anarchy, a chaotic period in English history marred by a civil war fought between King Stephen, a grandson of William the Conqueror, and his cousin and rival the Empress Matilda. In the centuries that followed, the Norman castle was added to, partly demolished, and then added to again, until a fire broke out during the time of the Restoration and destroyed most of the structure. The third Viscount Ashe, a great favorite of King Charles II and owner of the castle, as well as some thirty thousand acres of profitable farmland, decided to abandon the ruined fortress and build a new and more comfortable dwelling north of the ancient site. The result was the present structure, a fifty-room country estate surrounded by more than one thousand acres of game-filled woodland, which was designed for every pleasure and equipped with every convenience a seventeenth-century gentleman could buy.

Charlotte had lived at Ramblewood (she did not care to refer to herself as its mistress) during the first year of her marriage. But as her carriage swung into the gravel drive that led up to the house's majestic front entrance, her thoughts led her even further back, to the time she had first caught a glimpse of the towering portico, with its four soaring columns that were crowned by a massive carved pediment. For she had been introduced to her future husband at Ramblewood when, as a girl of seventeen, she had arrived at that imposing entranceway dressed in a snowy white silk gown and with a demure but costly string of pearls about her neck.

Her grandfather and Mrs. Seymour had been at her side when she entered the Great Hall where a ball given for the county's gentry was already in progress. Her young girl's dreams had still been firmly enthroned in her heart as her eyes eagerly took in the sight of the elegantly dressed men and women, who were gracefully executing the intricate steps of the dance. The brilliance of the candlelight and the sweet strains of the music had dazzled her senses and made her a captive of her imagination. She felt as if she had been magically transported from the kind but humdrum world at Hopewell to a new world that was all charm, beauty, and excitement.

But that was a lifetime ago.

On this day, the day before her husband's funeral, a drizzling rain was falling. A servant had already hurried out of the house to open the door to the carriage. Charlotte, still dressed in black and wearing only a small jet brooch as ornamentation, stepped down from the carriage, followed by Mrs. Seymour. When they were inside, another servant led them up the carpeted stone staircase and showed them to their rooms.

"Lady Cunningham is resting, my lady," said the servant, to explain the absence of a more dignified reception. "Dinner will be served at six." The servant then glanced uncertainly at Charlotte and added, "That is the hour when Lord and Lady Cunningham are accustomed to dine."

"Six o'clock will be fine," Charlotte replied. She knew Lady Cunningham, who had grown up at Ramblewood, had moved back into the home and assumed the role of mistress of the sprawling estate after Charlotte had returned to Hopewell. At the time, Charlotte had not really cared. She was happier in her own home. Her husband, who never had been interested in the estate's management, was happy to spend his time in London, or Brighton, or visiting the estates of his friends, where he was always a welcome guest. If Lady Cunningham preferred to live in Ramblewood, rather than in Lord Cunningham's humbler estate near Whitby, who was Charlotte to complain? It was better to have someone from the family living at the home, rather than to let it fall into gradual disrepair.

And so her arrival at Ramblewood was awkward only for the servants. Should they defer to her wishes, since she was the widow of Lord Ashe? Or should they continue to treat Lady Cunningham as the mistress of the place? Charlotte decided to resolve the issue for them by saying, "Please continue as usual while we are here, which will not be long. Mrs. Seymour and I plan to leave shortly after the funeral."

The servant curtseyed and left Ella to unpack their things. While Ella did so, Charlotte and Mrs. Seymour retired to the sitting room that adjoined Charlotte's bedroom. It was Charlotte's own sitting room — Lord and Lady Cunningham had chosen rooms in a different wing for their personal use — but the room's associations were not happy ones. She was therefore glad when a servant brought in some light refreshments and she could busy herself with filling her aunt's plate with sandwiches and small cakes. But not even the sight of the silver teapot, usually so welcome on a cold and rainy day, could smooth the ruffled feathers of Charlotte's companion.

"A governess would have received a more civil welcome," fumed Mrs. Seymour.

"What does it matter?" Charlotte replied. "After the funeral, we shall not have to see them again."

"But to treat you like a … a…"

"Penniless relation? Is that not what I am? I suppose I shall have to become used to these slights after we return to …" She could not finish the sentence. For the first time it struck her that she had no home to return to, and she was afraid. "Auntie, where shall we go? Where shall we live?"

"We must settle that issue with Lord and Lady Cunningham. You shall not leave this house until you have retrieved part of your lost money. Do not accept less than five thousand pounds."

"I will not accept anything from them, even if they were to offer."

"Charlotte, you must be sensible. Five thousand pounds invested in the funds will give you an income of two hundred and fifty a year. My income is two hundred a year. We could live on our two incomes, if we economize. But we cannot live on my income alone."

"I can work."

"My dear niece, those are fine words, but you have never had to work. You do not know what it means."

Charlotte thought back to Brighton and Mrs. Barker. Was that what the future had in store for her? To live out her days hovering on the margin of respectability, terrified that one day she would fall into the abyss?

"What if they do not offer to assist me?" asked Charlotte.

"Then you must demand it."

"Auntie, I cannot grovel before such people."

"Of course, you cannot. It is they who must grovel before you and attempt to make amends."

"Why should they do that?"

"Charlotte, for once listen to me and do not ask so many questions! You must not see yourself as a penniless relation, not even for a moment. When you married Lord Ashe, you were an heiress who brought fifty thousand pounds to the marriage, as well as the plantation in Jamaica and the estate at Hopewell, which were both promised to Lord Ashe after the demise of your grandfather. Your grandfather handed over the life and happiness of his only grandchild into the hands of a young lord who was unworthy of such a solemn trust.

You have been wronged. Wronged! And the family must pay."

VIII.

When Charlotte went down to dinner she was surprised to see that Lord March was in the drawing room, speaking to Lady Cunningham. Then she realized there was no cause for surprise. Lord March had accompanied her husband's coffin to Ramblewood. It would have been more surprising if he had not remained for the funeral.

Mrs. Seymour had come down before her and was attempting to make conversation with Lord Cunningham, who was doing nothing to make her task easier. Odelia Cunningham, a young lady of sixteen and the Cunninghams' only child, sat off to the side with a book. All eyes turned to Charlotte when she entered. But even though she had taken her aunt's words to heart and made an effort to dress her hair in a manner that was sufficiently heiress-like in appearance, only her aunt rewarded her with a smile. The others greeted her with looks that ranged from indifference to disapproval,

They all immediately went into the dining hall and the first course was served. As the dishes were passed around, Lord Cunningham and Lord March discussed the effects of the recent rains upon the summer crops. Lady Cunningham's conversation consisted of a series of heartfelt sighs, expressed in between taking small tastes of her food. Every once in a while she raised her handkerchief to her eyes, presumably to wipe away a tear.

Charlotte passed the desultory time by secretly observing Lord March, whenever such observation was possible. He was an impressive looking man for his age, which she guessed to be in his late thirties, in a country gentleman sort of way: sturdily built and with an intelligent face. His manners were polite and attentive, without being excessively so. When he spoke, it was to the point; and when he listened it was with evident interest to what Lord Cunningham was saying. All this, combined with the man's great wealth — for it was common knowledge the March family was one of the wealthiest in England — seemed to make a jest of the Bow Street Runner's suspicions. Such a man could not murder, Charlotte decided, unless he was provoked in a moment of passion. And what, she wondered, could provoke a man who seemed concerned only about sheep and drains to passion?

Mrs. Seymour, having no such thoughts to occupy her mind, for Charlotte had not revealed the details of her conversation with the Runner to her aunt, found it a torture to sit thus in silence. She therefore turned to Lady Cunningham and said, "It must be very difficult to have lost your brother."

"He was such a rare creature. So charming. So kind. It was impossible not to love him," replied Lady Cunningham, calling her handkerchief again into service.

Lord Cunningham turned his attention to his wife and said, "Do not distress yourself by talking, my dear. Tears will not bring him back."

"If only Ashe had married someone more appreciative of his talents. Perhaps …" Lady Cunningham allowed her words to drift to that faraway place where broken dreams and dashed hopes were presumably stored.

Mrs. Seymour, recognizing the slight to Charlotte and unable to restrain her indignation, asked sweetly, "Are you referring to his talent for gambling or for drinking?"

Lady Cunningham, who had been in the middle of raising a crystal goblet to her lips, set down the glass so hard on the table that its contents splattered on the cloth. All signs of wistful regret had vanished, as she replied, "My brother was a gentleman, and he had a gentleman's high spirits. A wise woman would have found ways to direct Lord Ashe's high spirits into more suitable pursuits, instead of leaving the poor man to flounder alone in dangerous waters."

"Surely you are not blaming Lady Ashe for your brother's sordid life?" replied Mrs. Seymour.

"I do not blame the young lady," said Lady Cunningham, glancing coldly in Charlotte's direction. "But she clearly was not instructed properly in the duties of a wife by those who were in charge of her education. Now we have all had to pay the sad price for this negligence."

It took a few moments for Mrs. Seymour to realize it was she who had just been insulted. When it finally dawned upon her, she was ready with a retort. However, a swift kick under the table from Charlotte forced Mrs. Seymour to keep her remarks to herself.

The rest of the meal passed in more desultory silence. Afterward, Lady Cunningham retired to her room, complaining of a headache. Lord Cunningham and Lord March remained in the dining room with their port and their cigars. That left only Charlotte and Mrs. Seymour to accompany the young lady of the house to the drawing room for tea.

Odelia Cunningham, who was as beautiful as she was shy, did her best to play hostess. However, just a few minutes after Mrs. Seymour took a seat by the fire sleep overcame her and the needlework she had brought into the room slipped from her hands and onto the highly polished floor.

"Would you mind if I played?" asked Odelia. "I do not know if it is quite right to do such a thing, with poor Uncle Percy not yet buried. But I feel so sad and sometimes music does help."

"I understand," replied Charlotte. "Play, if you like. It will not disturb me."

Odelia sat at the pianoforte and began to play. Charlotte recognized the piece. The country orchestra had been playing it when she had arrived for the first time at Ramblewood. Almost without her knowing it, she walked over to the half-open door that led to the Great Hall, which on happier occasions had served as the ballroom. The hall was dark, for no one was in it, but in Charlotte's mind's eye she could see it ablaze with light. The dance was in progress, in the center of the room. At one end sat the musicians, at the other sat the elderly ladies, who fanned themselves as they talked and sipped their lemonade.

Lord Cunningham, four years younger, had come forward, smiling and bowing to Charlotte and her grandfather and Mrs. Seymour. Then he called out, "Ashe, come greet your guests from Hopewell."

A young man turned his head and separated himself from the circle of friends that was gathered around him. While he walked toward them, Charlotte had ample time to study his features. If Lord Ashe was not perfectly handsome, he was possessed of a ready smile and an easy grace that more than made up for any minor defect. Indeed, Charlotte's young and inexperienced heart was won even before the young man greeted her grandfather and Mrs. Seymour with a hospitable show of respect, despite their differences in rank.

Lord Ashe chatted politely with her grandfather for a few moments about the condition of the roads. Then Lord Cunningham interjected, saying, "This is a ball. We must not keep the young people from their pleasures. Mrs. Seymour, may I offer you a glass of lemonade, or perhaps you would prefer a ratafia?"

Lord Cunningham deftly led away her two chaperons, leaving Charlotte alone with Lord Ashe. As if she was in a dream, she was aware of him leading her onto the dance floor, where a new set was beginning. She was vaguely aware that others were watching them, just as she was vaguely aware of the fact that Lord Ashe was making pleasant conversation and that somehow she was answering him. Yet it was as if she was seeing and hearing and talking and dancing while being enfolded within a soft, happy, and protecting cloud. Through that cloud she saw her grandfather and Mrs. Seymour, who were talking with Lord and Lady Cunningham. They all smiled at her. She smiled back. At that moment her fate was sealed. She knew it, and she was happy.

She was no fool. She knew the smiles of Lord and Lady Cunningham were so freely given because her grandfather was willing to freely give all of his great fortune to the man fortunate enough to win the hand of his only grandchild. But she was sure the smile of her future husband was genuine. If there was not yet love, for she knew real affection was something that only came with time, with years of experiencing both the joys and sorrows of a full life together, she felt sure there was at least a sincere willingness to begin to love, to care.

But if that smile had been sincere, who was responsible for what happened later, when the gauzy cloud disappeared and cold reality set in? Was it Lord and Lady Cunningham who had been at fault for knowingly selling damaged goods to her unsuspecting grandfather, who had been so dazzled by the old and distinguished title that he had neglected to inquire about the Viscount's character? Or was she the one who had destroyed the marriage, as Lady Cunningham had suggested at dinner, by being too quick to judge and condemn her young husband for his faults, while forgetting the good qualities which he also possessed?

"You are crying, Lady Ashe. My playing has disturbed you."

Charlotte turned. Odelia Cunningham was standing by her side. A concerned expression was on the young girl's face. Charlotte hastily removed her handkerchief and wiped away the tears that had fallen, unbeknownst to her, upon her cheeks.

"Perhaps we should retire," said Odelia Cunningham, as she closed the door that led to the Great Hall. "I do not think the gentlemen will join us this evening."

IX.

The next morning continued damp and gloomy. Through her bedroom window Charlotte saw that a heavy mist had rolled down from the heavens, where it conspired with a finer mist that had risen from the ground. The garden was barely visible, while the woods were concealed in a grey shroud. The moors were often like that, even in June.

The inclement weather provided a topic for breakfast, which might otherwise have been endured in an uneasy silence. Mr. Inkerwell, who had stayed in the village with a legal acquaintance, joined them for the meal. Afterward, the three men retired to the library, while Lady Cunningham went to inquire after the funeral biscuits and burnt wine, which were to be distributed to the servants, villagers, and other mourners who joined the funeral procession.

Charlotte and Mrs. Seymour were once again left to their own devices, but the meeting in the library did not take long. When Mr. Inkerwell joined them in the drawing room, he wore a grim look on his face. Coming straight to the point, as was his way, he said, "The family has agreed to settle upon you, Lady Ashe, a sum of four thousand pounds."

"We shall accept nothing less than five," Mrs. Seymour exclaimed.

"They claim they cannot be so generous."

"Cannot? Will not, I think you mean. Look at this house," and there Mrs. Seymour made a grand gesture. "Does this house have the look of a poor man's abode?"

"You have touched upon the exact problem," replied Mr. Inkerwell. "It has not yet been proved conclusively that Lord Ashe's death was due to murder, and not suicide. In addition, the family has not yet come to an end of Lord Ashe's debts. If the family loses Ramblewood, they will have lost a considerable amount of their wealth."

"Then I am surprised Lady Cunningham is willing to be so generous, under the circumstances," said Charlotte.

"It is not Lady Cunningham who is being generous. It is the Dowager Lady March who will be your benefactress."

Charlotte took a deep breath. "Well, Auntie, at least now I know why she stared at me like I was a cow on sale at market day. She was calculating the lowest price to buy me off."

"I am sorry, Lady Ashe," said Mr. Inkerwell. "I can understand how distressing this must be for you. But Lady March is not obliged to provide you with an income, and so it was difficult for me to press her son for more money."

"I am glad you did not. Indeed, you may tell Lord March that his mother need not concern herself about me. I have no need for her alms."

"Charlotte!" exclaimed Mrs. Seymour.

"We shall manage, Auntie, with what we have. I shall not be anyone's charity case."

Charlotte left the room, before the others could try to convince her to change her mind. Mrs. Seymour shook her head mournfully and said, "What shall we do, Mr. Inkerwell? How shall we live on my two hundred a year?"

"I shall inquire in Butterhill about cottages that might be available."

Mrs. Seymour allowed a low groan to escape from her lips. Butterhill was the Yorkshire village closest to Hopewell. It consisted of one main street and a few narrow lanes that wandered to nowhere in particular.

"If only we could live in Whitby," said Mrs. Seymour. "At least in Whitby there is life."

"I fear Charlotte would find it difficult to live in a busy port town like Whitby, even if she did not have to live on such a reduced income," replied Mr. Inkerwell, who felt comfortable enough in Mrs. Seymour's presence to refer to his client by the name he had called her by when she was a young girl. "She is a child of the moors."

Their conversation was interrupted by the sounds of the horses and carriages pulling into the drive. Through the window they could see several servants loading the coffin bearing Lord Ashe's remains into the largest of the carriages.

"The best thing would be if Charlotte remarried," said Mr. Inkerwell, as two servants covered the coffin with a large black cloth.

"How will she find a suitable husband, sir, if she is hidden away in a place like Butterhill? Pray, answer me that?"

X.

The road leading to the nearby village was almost totally obscured from the eye by the mist, but the coachmen and horses had traveled along that path many times before and so they needed but little direction. When the carriages reached the spot where the private drive met with the public road, a small crowd of mourners from the village and surrounding farms were waiting and they silently formed a procession behind the family's carriages.

The sound of carriage wheels approaching brought the minister outside the parish church, where he stood all solemn and obsequious. The service did not take long. The lords and ladies in attendance did not disgrace their rank by showing any emotion, and only a few of the older servants and villagers, who remembered the dead lord when he was a child, cried during the service. Then the casket was lowered into the ground, and the minister assured whoever was listening that the deceased would surely be resurrected to eternal life. The minister next invited Lord Cunningham and Lord March to each sprinkle a handful of earth into the open grave, which they did, in silence.

After the service was over, Mr. Inkerwell whispered a few words to Lord March and then joined Charlotte and Mrs. Seymour in the carriage that was to take them to Hopewell. While still in Brighton the solicitor had been able to ascertain that the new owner would not move in until the following week. The two ladies were therefore invited to stay at Hopewell for a few nights, to pack their personal belongings and make arrangements for new lodgings.

Charlotte did not look back at the little family group that remained in conversation outside the church. Instead, she kept her eyes firmly fixed on the shadowy landscape that passed before the carriage's window. The road they were traveling on was a country road, and so it twisted and turned through the moors according to a meandering logic of its own. But she did not mind. Each turn was taking her further away from Ramblewood.

"It is over," she whispered to no one in particular.

As if in answer to her thoughts, the clouds suddenly parted and a strong shaft of sunlight revealed a green patch of farmland dotted with a flock of sheep, which gazed lazily after the swiftly passing carriage. Charlotte gazed back with delight, letting her eye wander up to the top of the rolling hills, which glistened from the dew of their morning showers. At the top of one of those hills she could see a man on horseback. He seemed to be waiting for the carriage to pass by. She did not know why, but something about the lone figure made her feel uneasy.

"Mr. Inkerwell," she said, turning to the solicitor. He was fast asleep. Her aunt had also dozed off, in her corner of the carriage. Charlotte therefore returned her gaze to the window. But the horse and rider were gone, and in a few minutes the hilltop had disappeared from sight, too.

CANTO THE SECOND

When Charlotte and Mrs. Seymour arrived at Hopewell, there was no need to agonize over which favorite pieces of furniture to take and which to leave behind, or sort through the books in the library. They were allowed to remove only their clothing and other personal possessions. Even the china and serving dishes were no longer theirs.

While they supervised the packing of their trunks, Mr. Inkerwell traveled to Butterhill, where he made discreet inquiries concerning a suitable place for the two ladies to live. His discretion was wasted. The entire village had already heard the news and could speak of little else. Furthermore, only one dwelling was available for rent: a cottage that sat by itself in a small wood, but was still within easy walking distance of the village.

Mr. Inkerwell noted, with his solicitor's eye, that the advantages of the cottage were several. Its seclusion would shelter Charlotte from having to endure daily the prying eyes of the curious villagers and tenant farmers. And because the cottage was situated next to a pretty tributary of the River Esk — indeed, the cottage had been bought and furnished with an eye toward renting it to gentlemen in search of a few weeks communing with the picturesque — he hoped the gentle scene would help soften the blow of cottage living for one who had been accustomed to living on a much more expansive scale. As for the furnishings, they were not luxurious but at least they were clean and in good condition. And last, but certainly not the least of the cottage's good points, the chimney did not smoke.

The chief drawback was that the cottage was owned by Ella's brother, a hardworking young man who was well on his way to making his mark in the small corner of the world where he made his home. Alfred, for that was the young man's name, was encouraged by Ella to be generous in his dealings with the former mistress of Hopewell, and he was a shrewd enough businessman to calculate that if the Wheel of Fortune had turned once, it might very well turn again and restore the lady to a position of wealth, title, and benevolent patronage. Alfred therefore insisted on renting the cottage at a ridiculously low price, an offer which Mr. Inkerwell gratefully accepted. But since Mr. Inkerwell did not know how two ladies of sensibility would adjust to this reversal of roles, he paid the young man six months rent out of his own pocket, so Charlotte would be in his debt, and not in debt to a farmer.

On their last day at Hopewell, Charlotte bade farewell to the servants and paid them a month's wages, a feat that was accomplished through the sale of an emerald necklace, which had also been discreetly arranged by Mr. Inkerwell. The solicitor then conveyed the two ladies to the cottage in his own carriage. However, he refused Charlotte's invitation to stay for tea, claiming he was needed back in his office. Privately, he rightly assumed Charlotte had no wish to entertain visitors during her first day in her new home. He even detained Mrs. Seymour for several minutes in conversation, so Charlotte could have a few quiet moments to adjust to her new circumstances.

And so Charlotte was quite alone when she pushed open the heavy wood door and stepped inside the cottage for the first time. The front room was airy and spacious, and the sight of two comfortable chairs seated before the hearth — where logs had already been neatly prepared for the evening's fire — brought a smile to her lips. It would be possible to live in such a room, she decided. The smile faded, though, as she explored the rest of the cottage, for there was not much else to explore. In addition to the parlour, there were only two small bedchambers and a kitchen, and then she was already standing at the back door.

By this time, she heard the sound of the front door closing and footsteps that traveled the same path her own had taken just minutes before. The footsteps were silenced when her aunt came into the kitchen and stood beside her.

"It is quiet here," Charlotte remarked to her aunt, as they both surveyed the wooded scene that lay beyond the cottage's small back garden. "We shall not be bothered, and that is a blessing."

"The front room is pleasant," replied Mrs. Seymour, doing her best to be cheerful. "Only I do wish we could have brought along one of the carpets. The one in the library would have added warmth to the room."

"At least we have been spared the sight of seeing Hopewell emptied of everything that made it such a pleasant home," said Charlotte, who did not wish to be reminded of the comforts she had left behind.

"Do you really think Mr. Collins will redo the house? If he does, I hope he is a man of moderate tastes. I could not bear the thought of Hopewell done up in the Egyptian style."

"Most likely that will depend upon the taste of Mrs. Collins."

"I suppose you are right." Mrs. Seymour then added, "Charlotte, it was very good of you to sell your necklace to pay the servants their wages. Your grandfather would have been very proud."

"I shall not need an emerald necklace in Butterhill."

"You talk as though you shall never again go to a ball."

"I do not expect to receive invitations to parties at fine houses, now that I no longer have fifty thousand pounds to bestow upon some fortunate gentleman."

"But surely the county gentry will not entirely forget us. And you cannot intend to turn recluse."

"No, but I must learn to be happy in my new circumstances. Shall I help you unpack? Which bedchamber do you prefer?"

Charlotte returned to the small passageway that led to the two bedchambers. Mrs. Seymour followed. But as she gazed at the two tiny rooms, which each had room for only a bed, a small closet, and a wash basin, Mrs. Seymour could only say, "I do wish the cottage did not belong to Ella's family. To think we have been reduced to being the tenants of a former servant."

"We must not think, Auntie. Otherwise, we shall go mad."

II.

While Charlotte was still helping her aunt unpack, there was a knock at the back door and then a voice called out, "It is only me, my lady. Ella."

By the time Charlotte reached the kitchen, which did not take long, given the smallness of the cottage, Ella was already in the process of lighting a fire.

"Supper will be ready as soon as I boil up the water for the tea," said Ella.

Charlotte noticed on the table a large basket that had not been sitting there before. She correctly guessed the basket was filled with food for their supper, and probably food for the next day, as well.

"I will pay you for the food and your trouble of bringing it here," said Charlotte, "but you are not to light the fire or make our tea. You have been discharged, Ella. I cannot afford to keep a servant anymore."

"Did not Mr. Inkerwell tell you, my lady?"

"Tell me what?"

"The terms of the rental agreement include a day servant to keep the cottage neat and tidy, and bring in food from the village, and wait at table, and brush the clothes."

"Mr. Inkerwell said nothing at all," Charlotte replied, assuming her sternest-sounding voice.

Ella sighed. "Then my brother must have forgotten to tell him. Alfred's a good-hearted soul, but sometimes he cannot remember if it is a market day or a Sunday, and he does look a sight when he's wearing his Sunday best to buy a cow."

Ella scooped up a few plates and some pieces of cutlery and, after giving her mistress a curtsey, went into the front room to lay the table. During the meal, she deftly kept a steady stream of conversation flowing while she served the dishes, informing Charlotte and Mrs. Seymour about what vegetables could be grown in the garden and where the best fishing was in the nearby stream. Although Mrs. Seymour declared she should never pick up a rod and do combat with a live and thrashing fish, Charlotte surprised her aunt by stating that she intended to try her luck before the week was out.

"There are also many pretty places to sketch," Ella added. "At least a gentleman who rented the cottage seemed to think so."

"The last renter was a painter?" asked Mrs. Seymour, who was feeling much more at peace with the cottage after having eaten a good meal. "It is a pity he did not leave behind any of his paintings to adorn the walls."

"He was here last summer," Ella replied. "The last renters were poets."

Mrs. Seymour replaced her teacup on its saucer. "Poets?"

"At least I think they were poets, Ma'am. My brother told me they slept until noon and wore knotted kerchiefs around their throats, as that Lord Byron is said to do. But Alfred said he did not recall ever seeing more than one or two scraps of paper lying on the table, so perhaps they were not poets after all."

"I hope they were not. If I had known there were poets in Butterhill, I should have spoken to your brother."

"Auntie," said Charlotte, who was very aware of Mrs. Seymour's prejudice concerning gentlemen who rhymed, "I am sure they did nothing worse than write bad verse."

"You may laugh, Charlotte, at an old woman's ideas. But in my day, no self-respecting gentleman would spend his time stanzifying."

"Milton was a poet."

"Milton was a clergyman. And Milton was born two hundred years ago. He was hardly my contemporary."

"Let us not argue," said Charlotte. "If we cannot have elegance in our cottage, at least we can have peace."

"Very well," replied Mrs. Seymour, pouring out the last of the tea into their teacups. "But I do not see why we cannot have both. We have our sewing boxes, and you have your paints. We have only to make a plan, and this room shall soon be transformed."

And so the first evening passed, and the time passed much more cheerfully than Charlotte had hoped or expected.

III.

For the next few days the two ladies were busy with their needles. But even though they got on well together, it was difficult for both of them to adjust to the continual bumping into one another. At Hopewell, they had met for meals, spent the morning and evening doing needlework, and taken an afternoon stroll around the garden. But there had also been ample space to engage in more solitary pursuits at other hours of the day.

At the cottage there was no such opportunity for escape. Therefore, on a morning when the weather was especially fine, Charlotte decided to both make good on her promise of trying her luck with the fish and indulge in a few hours of uninterrupted solitude. Cheerfully announcing that she was setting out for the stream, she grasped in one hand the fishing rod that a previous occupant of the cottage had left behind. In her other hand she held an empty straw basket that, she laughingly promised, would be filled with fish when she returned.

The art of fishing was not totally unknown to her. Her grandfather had enjoyed the sport, and when she was a child he sometimes took her with him to the stream that rambled through Hopewell's gently sloping meadows. While he waded in the water, she had spent her time chasing after butterflies or following the calls of the corncrakes. But when it was time to open the picnic hamper, she would run back to the riverbank and join her grandfather for a light meal. As they dined upon the delicacies that had been prepared by their faithful Cook, Charlotte would ask her grandfather to tell her stories about her parents, who had died in Jamaica from the fever, and the sugar plantation where she was born.

Sometimes he would let her hold the rod, too, cautioning, "Patience, Charlotte. Don't tug at the line. Wait and the fish will come to you."

And so on that fine June morning she cast her line into the clear waters of the stream and forced herself to wait, not because she really believed any fish would be so foolish as to take her inexpert bait, but because she knew she needed to be patient. Her life had not turned out as she had expected, yet she still retained a small reservoir of hope that all was not as bleak as it seemed.

She wondered what, if anything, Theo Bryght had discovered in Brighton. If she had been a man, she would have returned to that town to conduct her own inquiries. But how could she go into a gambling establishment and question the club's members? They would think her mad, or worse.

Of course, if Lady March could see her on this morning, by the river and with a fishing rod in her hand, the sight would surely give the older woman an excellent reason to raise her quizzing glass to her eye and stare. Charlotte smiled at the thought. But knowing she was perfectly alone, she did not care. She could do as she pleased, and so she decided to practice her casting technique, even though she had no idea of what a proper technique was. That did not bother her, either, since who was there to judge? And so after raising the rod as high above her head as she could, she cast it behind her with a great force, intending to throw it back into the stream. But when she made a movement to bring the rod forward, the line got tangled on a branch, an event that made her unexpectedly tug and turn — and gasp.

"Beg your pardon, Ma'am," said Lord March, who was standing on the top of the river bank, just a few feet away. "I did not mean to alarm you. Mrs. Seymour said you would be here." He then came down towards her and, having taken the rod from her hand, he began to disentangle the line.

"My grandfather used to say that fishing is a wonderful healer for the soul," Charlotte said by way of reply, trying to hide her intense embarrassment. It had been one thing to flaunt convention in front of an imaginary Dowager, and quite another to be caught prancing around with a fishing rod in her hand, and with her husband only recently buried, by a very real Lord March.

"I have found that to be true myself," replied Lord March, who was politely keeping his attention on the line to give Charlotte time to regain her composure, a courtesy for which she silently thanked him.

"I hope Lady March is well," Charlotte said, since she did not know how else to break the silence.

"She was in excellent health when I last saw her in Brighton."

The fishing line being now untangled, Lord March handed the rod back to Charlotte. Looking into her eyes for the first time, he added, "We were not able to speak privately in Brighton, or at Ramblewood. As I felt it was important for you to know what I have learned about your husband's death, I took the liberty of coming here."

"Do you know who murdered my husband?"

"No. And I cannot even say for sure that Lord Ashe was murdered. I leave the facts of Lord Ashe's death to that Runner from London to discover. I came here only to warn you."

"Warn me?"

"I have made inquiries concerning the person who acquired Hopewell."

"I believe the gentleman's name is Mr. John Collins," she replied, trying not to reveal the emotion she felt whenever it was necessary to mention the name of Hopewell's new owner.

"The man's name is Collins, but he is not a gentleman. He served as your late husband's valet during the Peninsular Campaign."

Charlotte was momentarily too shocked to speak. Part of her hated the class distinctions that were so dear to the English aristocracy. When her grandfather left England, he had left it as the younger son of a tradesman, and even when he returned as a wealthy plantation owner he still lacked what the city gentry called "polish." Yet she was sure he had been a better man than many of the gentlemen who considered idleness to be a virtue and living on credit an unalienable right. But the thought that a former valet was now the master of Hopewell was a chasm too wide for even her to cross.

"I do not understand, Lord March. It is my understanding Mr. Collins won Hopewell in a bet. Is it not true that gentlemen's gambling clubs have rules for who is permitted to enter the club and play?"

"They do have such rules. But Mr. Collins entered the club as a friend of Lord Ashe."

"I cannot believe that. My husband did not treat his servants as his friends."

"Mr. Collins was no longer your husband's servant. It seems his fortunes took a turn for the better after he left the army and returned to England. I have not yet learned how his fortune was acquired. But I have discovered that more than once he did your late husband the favor of paying off an IOU."

"That was a kindness, was it not?"

"One would like to think so."

"Yet you feel it necessary to warn me about this man?"

"It is one thing to pay a gambling debt of a few hundred pounds, and quite another to play for stakes worth an entire estate. I cannot help but wonder how Mr. Collins accomplished this feat."

"My solicitor saw the transfer of ownership. It looked to be perfectly in order."

"Your husband died not long after he wrote it."

"Even if Mr. Collins is somehow implicated in this matter, I do not see what else Mr. Collins can do to harm me. My husband is dead. My fortune and estate are lost. What more can he, or anyone, take from me?"

"The object you found in the snuff box."

Charlotte was glad she had the rod to hold on to, for the act of holding it helped to steady her trembling hands as the suspicions raised by the Runner came back to her in a rush. *Why had Lord March been so interested in her husband's death?*

She then recalled the ungenerous offer of the four thousand pounds. Were they trying to buy her silence, and at the cheapest possible price? she wondered.

Waves of fear and humiliation washed over her, and she could only hope Lord March would attribute the rising colour in her cheeks to the hotness of the day. She tried to calm her emotions by reminding herself that Lord March might be perfectly innocent — his interest in the box might be due only to the interest he had seen *her* express in it. But instead of calming her, this new thought only caused more distress. For even if Lord March were innocent of murder, she would not be humiliated by this family again, she decided. She would not reveal to them the shaming secret that her husband had been in love with another woman. And so raising her eyes to meet his, she said, "The box was empty. You saw it was empty with your own eyes."

Lord March considered her for a few moments. Then he said, "If I may be so bold as to offer an opinion, you have lost your opportunity. The day has grown hot, and the fish are gone. Good day, Lady Ashe."

IV.

That night Charlotte dreamed about fish. But unlike her daytime excursion, the river of her dreams was filled with swarms of silvery trout that glided through the cascading waters that tumbled over the rocky course. She had only to cast her line and dozens of them swam forward to eagerly swallow the bait. Her basket was soon filled to overflowing. A servant removed it and set another in its place.

Another servant took the basket to a long table, where Ella and Cook, the one from her childhood, were laughing and conversing while they cleaned the mounds of fish that were stacked high all around them.

What's all this? Cook called out, as she pulled something shiny out of a gaping mouth.

It's a locket! Ella replied. *There's a locket in that fish!*

Cook held the silvery locket up to the sun, so it glinted in the light. The servants and the villagers — and suddenly there was a great rush of people — surged forward to see the shiny orb, which seemed to glow brighter and brighter with each turn on its chain. Lady Cunningham was there, too, pushing her way through the crowd. Charlotte also wanted to reach the locket, so she could grab it from Cook's hand and secret it away. But she stood rooted to her spot near the stream, like one of the trees that lined the shore. Even the ribbons of her bonnet had become entangled in the twigs and leaves.

From that distance, she watched while the crowd fought to win the prize. The battle grew fierce, and blood began to flow. At last one man clawed and climbed his way to the top and snatched away the locket. When it was in his hand, the crowd melted away, as though they had never existed.

The man turned and, slipping the locket into his waistcoat's pocket, showed her his face. It was her husband, Lord Ashe.

Beg your pardon, Ma'am, he said, smiling. *I did not mean to alarm you.*

V.

When Charlotte awoke there were tears in her eyes, and those tears made her angry. She knew it was madness to argue with a dream, but she could not help but be irritated with Lord Ashe. If he must appear in her dreams, she wished he would come with the letter he had written on the night of his death.

Then it occurred to her that perhaps she was not being fair. If she wished to dream of letters at night, she should not go fishing during the day. She should write a letter, or a poem, if Mrs. Seymour was not about. If she felt more ambitious, she might even try her hand at writing a novel. But the important thing was to write, and then see what materialized in her dreams. This thought cheered her up, and by the time she had dressed, she felt sufficiently in control of her emotions to suggest an excursion to the village.

"Why, Charlotte?" asked Mrs. Seymour. "Ella can purchase whatever we need."

"We must face the villagers sometime. The sooner we do so, the sooner the gossip will stop. And I need to buy some writing paper. I might take your advice and write a novel."

As Mrs. Seymour could hardly dissuade her niece from following her own advice, after breakfast she reluctantly went to fetch her bonnet. Her humour did not improve when they were outside, even though the walk to the village was a pleasant one. But when they reached the village, and the prospect of new people to converse with became palpable, Mrs. Seymour became more cheerful. While she went to the apothecary's shop to purchase a bottle of Milk of Roses, for her complexion, Charlotte went to purchase her writing paper. When Charlotte returned to the apothecary, she found her aunt in deep consultation with the shop's owner.

"You were right to insist on taking a walk this morning, my dear," said Mrs. Seymour, who had turned at the sound of the jangling of the little bell that hung over the shop's doorway. "A set of watercolours was delivered to Butterhill by mistake, and they are of the very best quality. If you do not want them, Mr. Hearn shall send them back to London with the mail coach. Shall he wrap them up for you?"

Charlotte was about to give her assent, for her own stock of paints was running low, when she recalled that her personal allowance might not be sufficient for both paints and paper. She therefore hesitated, and in those few moments she thought she could see the apothecary take note of her confusion. She also had the feeling that the other person in the shop, a gentleman, was listening to her conversation with some interest, even though his back was turned toward her.

"I shall take them with me, Mr. Hearn," she said, unable to bear the thought of it becoming known in the village that Lady Ashe could no longer afford a set of paints.

"Yes, Lady Ashe."

The apothecary wrapped the paints, and when he was done he wrote a few numbers on the paper, which Charlotte correctly understood was the price of her purchase. She calmly removed the coins from her purse and placed them on the counter, although inwardly she was in shock the paints had cost so much.

"Shall we go, Mrs. Seymour?" she said to her aunt, who had crossed to the other side of the shop, where she was gazing intently at an advertisement for Newton's Restorative Tooth Powder.

While Charlotte waited for her aunt to join her at the door, the apothecary turned his attention to the gentleman, who had taken her place at the counter. "Do you live in these parts, sir?" asked Mr. Hearn. "I do not believe I have had the pleasure of making your acquaintance."

"I live at Hopewell," the man replied. "I am the new owner." He then turned, as though he knew Charlotte would be staring at him and bowed his head slightly in her direction. Charlotte nodded her head in return, for she had been staring, since she was certain this was Mr. Collins.

The word "Hopewell" had made Mrs. Seymour quickly rush to Charlotte's side, and so they were able to make a dignified retreat from the shop. Once they were out on the pavement, though, Mrs. Seymour began to search frantically through her reticule.

"What are you looking for?" Charlotte whispered between clenched teeth.

"My vinaigrette. I am going to faint."

"You shall do nothing of the sort," Charlotte replied, taking her aunt by the arm and forcing the woman to walk quickly with her down the road.

"But Charlotte —"

"I did not faint when I saw the price of paints I had no wish to buy, and you shall not faint at our unexpected meeting of Mr. Collins."

"There is no comparison. You never faint. I, on the other hand, have a delicate constitution." Mrs. Seymour, realizing that in truth the crisis had already passed, now they were in the open air, glanced sheepishly at her niece and added, "Where the paints shockingly expensive?"

"They were."

"I am sorry, Charlotte. I should have realized they would be, since they came all the way from Mr. Ackermann's Emporium in London."

They continued in silence, each wishing to speak of the topic that concerned them most — Mr. Collins — and both not knowing how to broach the subject to the other. When they returned to the cottage, Mrs. Seymour retired to her room to consider her complexion, which she was sure still bore traces of her recent shock. Charlotte got out the apron she wore when writing or painting, to protect her clothes from spills, and undid the package containing the paints. After she arranged the bottles on a small writing desk, she undid the wrapping of her package of paper.

Although she was anxious to try her writing experiment, the unexpected meeting with Mr. Collins combined with the sight of so many empty pages made the prospect of writing a novel, or even a poem, too daunting. She therefore thought she might write a letter to the Runner, to inform him of her meeting with Lord March. Yet she did not like to put down in writing the suspicions that had passed through her mind, since writing gave an unearned weight to thoughts that were as yet still as unsubstantial as air. Besides, Lord March had retuned to Lundsmoor Park, without attempting to see her again, which surely was proof she was in no danger from that quarter.

While she was considering who else she could write to her thoughts traveled back to the apothecary shop. She had caught just a glimpse of the face of Hopewell's new owner, hardly enough to form an impression of the man's character. Yet the chance meeting had, unfortunately, solidified in her mind something that she had been trying to avoid, the certain knowledge there were other people living in her former home. Perhaps at that very moment Mrs. Collins was arranging the flowers in the front drawing room or taking a walk in the shrubbery. Later she would join her husband in the dining room for the evening meal, which would be served on the heavy plate Charlotte's grandfather had purchased at a good price at an estate sale. After dinner, if the evening was chilly, a fire would be lit the sitting room. Perhaps Mr. Collins would read to his wife while she did her needlework. Or perhaps she would play the pianoforte while he read a newspaper.

Or perhaps they would do nothing of the sort. If he was a former valet, it was very likely Mrs. Collins was a former housemaid. Their amusements would not be her amusements, and Charlotte shuddered to think of the drinking parties and gaudy entertainments that might take place in Hopewell's stately halls.

She did not wish to hate Mr. and Mrs. Collins. She did not wish to stoop so low in her own esteem. But she knew the letter that she did wish to write:

You are not the new owner of Hopewell, Mr. Collins. Though you say it to the apothecary and the butcher and the baker, in my *eyes you will always be a valet who has overstepped his place.*

VI.

If Charlotte dreamed that night, she did not remember. When she was wakened by streams of sunlight cascading into her room, her mind felt dull and weary, as though an internal battle had been fought during the night without her knowing of it. A lingering sense of irritability accompanied her to the front room, where Mrs. Seymour was already busy at her work.

Neither her own workbasket nor the writing table held any allure for her, and so Charlotte wandered outside. Again her thoughts went to Brighton and the Bow Street Runner. It was so maddening not to know what progress was being made in the inquiry. If only there was something she could do in Butterhill. But what could she possibly discover in the sleepy village?

Her thoughts were interrupted by the sound of an approaching wagon. It was the gardener from Hopewell, who doffed his hat when he spotted Charlotte standing in front of the cottage.

"Compliments of Mr. Collins, my lady," he said to Charlotte, climbing down from the wagon. Then he bowed his head in the direction of Mrs. Seymour, who had also come outside to greet the gardener. "And Mr. Collins hopes my lady will not take it amiss that he has sent over these cuttings."

"How very kind," Mrs. Seymour said. "I wonder how Mr. Collins knew we so enjoyed our roses."

"I was showing Mr. Collins around the grounds," the gardener replied, "and let slip that my lady was partial to the rose garden for her afternoon walk. He then told me it was a shame there was no one to enjoy the garden now and that he shouldn't mind if I brought some cuttings to the cottage." The gardener, who was not used to speaking so much, paused before he asked, "Where should I plant them, my lady?"

"We shall take care of that," said Charlotte. "You are surely needed back at Hopewell."

"Begging your pardon, my lady, but Mr. Collins was very clear that I should bring my spade and plant the cuttings, so as not to cause you and Mrs. Seymour any trouble. Shall I take a look around the back?"

"I know just the spot," said Mrs. Seymour, leading the gardener to the back of the cottage. "There is one corner which gets very good sun for a good part of the day."

Charlotte decided to leave the planting of the cuttings in Mrs. Seymour's expert hands. Returning inside, she wandered over to the writing desk and sat down. She supposed Mr. and Mrs. Collins had meant well, but the gift had brought more trouble than pleasure. She would have to write to them, to thank them. But what if they, in turn, answered her letter with an invitation to come to Hopewell for tea?

The thought of having tea in her old home with a former valet and housemaid — for by this time she was sure Mrs. Collins must have been a servant, as well — made her turn to stone. Why had they made her a gift of the rose cuttings? she wondered. Why did they wish to make *her* acquaintance? The only possible reason was that they wished to use her to raise their standing in the area, not caring that by doing so they would be lowering her to their level.

But she would not let them do it. The shame that her husband had heaped upon her head she must submit to, having no other choice. This, though, was different. She would write Mr. and Mrs. Collins a brief note of thanks for the rose cuttings and ignore any further communication on their part.

Having made her decision, she went to the writing table to compose her letter. Then she stopped.

"What a fool I am being," she whispered. Had not Mr. Collins known her husband, and even gone so far as to pay some of her husband's debts? Was it not therefore probable he possessed information that might be useful in discovering the cause of her husband's death? He had been with Lord Ashe on the fatal night. He was known to at least some of her late husband's acquaintances and them to him. He was therefore knowledgeable about the state of their pocketbooks and the quality of their characters. She had only to gain the confidence of Mr. Collins and assure him of their mutual interest in clearing Lord Ashe's name and finding the perpetrator of the crime. In short, there was something she could do in Butterhill, after all!

But instead of picking up her pen to write, she jumped up from her seat and began to pace across the room. Prudence, she knew, would advise her to write one letter — for this was an excellent reason to write to the Bow Street Runner, advising the man that Mr. Collins was at present at Hopewell and it was perhaps time for the Runner to bring his inquiries to Yorkshire. Pride, though, was urging her to leave the Runner in Brighton, while she conducted her own inquiries in private. If she could discover pertinent information about the crime, without having to reveal to anyone else unfortunate details about her husband's private life, she could both cleanse her husband's reputation of its stain and leave her own reputation unsullied by scandal. So what was it to be, a letter to the Runner or to Mr. Collins? What was it to be?

As always, when her mind was in turmoil and she could not hope to find sound advice in the whirling stream of her own thoughts, she reached out her hand to poetry.

Meanwhile, Mrs. Seymour had instructed Ella to bring outside some refreshments for the gardener, who was surely thirsty after his drive to Butterhill. Ella, who understood Mrs. Seymour's intentions perfectly, brought the man a mug of cool ale, a maneuver that left Mrs. Seymour free to retire to the kitchen, where she could overhear the conversation between Ella and the gardener without revealing her interest in the matter.

"And how do your new master and mistress treat you, Luke?" Ella asked, after the gardener had taken a long drink of the ale.

"Mr. Collins ain't been no trouble," he replied. "As for the lady ..." He let the end of the sentence tumble into the depths of his mug, where it presumably met a premature death in the ale.

"A sharp one, is she? Has she given you a scold?"

Luke shook his head. "No. I never even seen her. No one has."

"What? Not even the day she arrived? You must have seen her when she stepped down from the carriage and said her hellos."

"I tell you, Ella, no one saw her face. The lady was all wrapped in some heavy kind of veil."

"How did she see to climb the stairs, then?"

"Her maid was with her. It was she who led the new lady to her room."

"Without a word to anyone?"

"Not a word then and not a word since."

"Not even at meals?" Ella persisted. "Not even to say, 'Tell Cook the soup is too salty'?"

"The lady don't come downstairs."

"Never?"

"Never."

Ella paused in her questioning to think this over. "The master will not let her, or she does not want to come?"

Luke laughed and said, "You're a shrewd one, Ella. The master said to Cook that his wife was sickly."

"Then that explains it."

"Does it, now? So why is there no doctor to attend her?"

"Perhaps by sickly Mr. Collins means something else. Perhaps the poor lady's face is terribly disfigured. You remember, Luke, don't you, what happened to the Lacey boy who was asleep in the barn when it caught fire?"

"Aye, we thought of that, too, Ella. That would explain the veil. But why don't she come outside? Why don't she leave her room? That's what some of us want to know."

Having finished his ale, and his supply of conversation, the gardener went back to work. Mrs. Seymour rushed into the front room, where she found her niece restlessly pacing up and down, reading aloud from a book of poems. She waited impatiently in the doorway until Charlotte paused for breath, frustrated to see that Charlotte was in one of her "moods" when she had so much interesting gossip to share. Meanwhile Charlotte, seemingly oblivious to her aunt's presence, enunciated with almost feverish excitement each word of the poem, which was titled "Ode to Solitude" and written by Alexander Pope, saying:

" 'How happy he, who free from care, The rage of courts, and noise of towns, Contented breathes his native air, In his own grounds. Whose herds with milk, whose fields with bread,

Whose flocks supply him with attire, Whose trees in summer yield him shade, In winter fire.' "

"Charlotte," Mrs. Seymour interrupted, impatient to get her niece's attention.

Charlotte glanced over at her aunt, and said, " '*Blest! …'* "

"What?"

" '*… who can unconcern'dly find, Hours, days, and years slide swift away, In health of body, peace of mind, Quiet by day,'* "

"I am sure I do not know. But …"

" '*Sound sleep by night; study and ease, Together mix'd; sweet recreation, And innocence, which most does please, With meditation. Thus let me live, unheard, unknown; Thus unlamented let me die; Steal from the world, and not a stone Tell where I lie.'*

"That is what I am trying to tell you."

"It is? You, too, wish to live unheard, unknown, and unlamented, like Mr. Alexander Pope? You surprise me, Auntie. I thought you wished to move to Whitby."

"I was not referring to myself. I was referring to Mrs. Collins."

"Mrs. Collins?"

"Yes, I have shocking news."

"Should I sit down? Are you about to tell me that Mrs. Collins writes verse? And I have just decided to write a letter inviting her and Mr. Collins to take tea with us tomorrow."

"I would not know what she writes, nor would anyone in Butterhill, seeing she is locked away in a solitary room. Can you imagine, Charlotte? None of the servants have seen her, not once. She does not even come downstairs to take her meals." Mrs. Seymour stopped in the middle of her recitation and stared at Charlotte. "Did you say you wish to invite Mrs. Collins to tea?"

"Yes."

"Then we shall meet her tomorrow!"

"Not if she does not leave her room. Is she ill?"

"That is what Mr. Collins would have us believe."

"But we do not believe him?"

"Certainly not! Luke said …" Mrs. Seymour stopped, embarrassed to have revealed she was repeating gossip overheard in the kitchen.

"I wonder what Luke is saying about us," said Charlotte. "It is so hard to live unheard and unknown when servants are about."

Mrs. Seymour chose to ignore this last remark and change the topic, saying, "Charlotte, do be serious. If Mrs. Collins is too ill to come to the cottage, we must set aside our pride and go to Hopewell. Perhaps she requires our assistance. It must be very uncomfortable to be ill in a strange house and in a neighborhood where one does not know a soul."

"So we do believe Mr. Collins?"

Mrs. Seymour, who was already envisioning an interesting excursion on the morrow, looked blankly at her niece. "This has nothing to do with belief," she replied in a solemn tone of voice she usually reserved for announcing the latest fashion dictates from Paris. "We must allow Mrs. Collins to speak for herself."

VII.

To Mrs. Seymour's relief and happiness, no letter of regret from Hopewell blackened her morning. She therefore assumed Mrs. Collins would arrive in the afternoon for tea and took upon herself the task of ordering Ella about the kitchen. Since Ella was already an expert at preparing scones and sponge cakes and paper-thin bread and butter sandwiches, after a short while

Mrs. Seymour felt it safe to leave the kitchen and attend to her toilette. When that task was done, she took a seat by the front window and waited for the carriage to arrive.

"She is here!" Mrs. Seymour called out at the same moment that the first sounds of the approaching carriage were heard. "Do come, Ella! You must open the door for Mrs. Collins!"

However, when the horses came to a halt and the groom sprung down from his perch and opened the door, no lady stepped down from the carriage. Only Mr. Collins emerged from the conveyance and walked up the path to the cottage's front door.

Mrs. Seymour, although disappointed, consoled herself with the thought that all was not lost. It would only be good manners to inquire after the health of the man's wife. From there, she would bring the conversation round to the topic of home remedies, a topic she was most knowledgeable about, and in this way draw out the pertinent details. And so when she appeared at Hopewell's door to visit the invalid, with several of those remedies in hand, it would seem the most natural thing in the world.

Mr. Collins, who saw only the smiling face of the older woman, allowed himself to be seated in the room's most comfortable chair. But almost as soon as he sat down Charlotte entered the room, causing him to jump up at once. This, in turn, caused him to bump into the writing desk, an act which sent several of the new bottles of watercolour paints crashing to the floor.

Charlotte could not entirely contain the gasp that had sprung to her lips as she watched the expensive paints combine into a muddy puddle. But when she saw the mottled face of their visitor, who appeared to be wishing that the floor would open under his feet and swallow him up, along with the mess, she regained her presence of mind and said, "Forgive me, Mr. Collins. It was foolish of me to leave the paints on that desk. I hope they have not soiled your coat."

"It is I who must ask your pardon, Lady Ashe."

"Perhaps we should see the garden, before tea is served. My aunt, Mrs. Seymour, has found the perfect place for the rose cuttings."

It did not take long to show Mr. Collins the garden. Even to an untrained eye, and Mr. Collins informed the ladies he was not an initiate in the mystery of growing roses and other blooms, it must look small and uninteresting in comparison to the landscaped grounds at Hopewell. Yet Mr. Collins's admission offered an opening to Mrs. Seymour, who asked, "Does Mrs. Collins enjoy a garden? We are so sorry she could not join us for tea."

"Mrs. Collins is ill," he replied, "and so she cannot supervise the gardening staff in their duties. But I am sure she takes great pleasure from looking at the gardens from her window."

"It is not a serious illness, we hope," Mrs. Seymour persisted.

"I am afraid it is."

Although Mr. Collins gave no sign of wishing to continue the conversation, Mrs. Seymour was not one to be put off so easily. And so she said, "The journey to Hopewell must have quite worn her out. I have a cordial that is just the thing to strengthen a person and restore their vitality, have I not, Charlotte? With your permission, Mr. Collins, I shall make a fresh batch and send some over to your wife."

"Thank you. I appreciate your concern, but I insist you do not go to so much trouble."

"It is no trouble at all, especially if it will do your wife good."

"It will not."

They had been strolling, aimlessly, around the garden, but now they stopped. During the brief conversation between Mrs. Seymour and Mr. Collins, Charlotte had taken the opportunity to study the young man, who appeared to be close to her age. Although he had not been born to the gentry, his speech revealed that he had apparently received an adequate education. If his manners were not as highly polished as a duke's pair of Hessian boots, they were on par with those of a country gentleman. His taste in clothes was admirably restrained for someone who had only recently come into a fortune. And, finally, she could not help but observe that he was exceptionally handsome.

For a few moments her imagination traveled back to Brighton, to the evening when he had entered the gaming establishment with her husband. It was very possible the regular visitors to the club mistook Lord Ashe's friend for the younger son of a viscount or baronet. No one who saw him would think he was a former valet, and even his speech had the air of one who was more accustomed to command than to obey.

"I apologize, Ma'am, for being so abrupt," he was saying to Mrs. Seymour, as Charlotte's thoughts returned to the present conversation. "My wife does not suffer from an illness of the body. It is her mind that has been destroyed. I hope that now you will understand why Mrs. Collins will neither be inviting you nor accepting your invitations to tea. Good day."

He strode off towards his carriage, which had remained in front of the cottage. Before he could reach it, Charlotte caught up with him. "Mr. Collins, do not be angry at us for inquiring into your personal affairs. I will not lie and say we were not curious. But when we heard your wife was unwell, my aunt did have a sincere desire to help."

The young man kept his gaze fixed upon the horses for a few moments. Then he said, stiffly, "My apologies, Lady Ashe, for misunderstanding your aunt's intentions."

"You are still angry. I can see it. But we are neighbours, and the village is too small for quarrels. Pray, let us be friends."

"Have you forgotten, Lady Ashe, that I am the one who stole Hopewell and left you without a home?"

Charlotte was silent. In those few moments — moments when she had been both pleasantly surprised by the young man's handsome looks and graceful manner and touched by his private sorrow — she had forgotten about Hopewell and the awkwardness of their situation. The fact that *he* had not forgotten only served to further raise him in her esteem. She therefore replied, "My husband gambled it away. If he had not lost it to you, he would have lost it to someone else."

"Someone else might have been in a position to be more generous. But I cannot afford to be generous. My wife must have a quiet place to live. She must be secluded so she will cause no harm to others. And so even though I understand how difficult it must be for you to live in this cottage, I cannot give you back the home you must love dearly."

"I have no expectation you would do such a thing."

"You are telling the truth?"

Charlotte raised her eyes to meet his. She saw that his eyes were a deep grey. It was like gazing into a moor on a misty day.

"Yes, you are telling me the truth. I can see it in your eyes, just as I can see the hurt and the pain. Life has not been kind to us, has it, Lady Ashe?"

"We can still be kind to others."

"Very well," he said, bowing slightly first to Charlotte and then to Mrs. Seymour. "If I am still invited …"

"Of course, you are, Mr. Collins," said Mrs. Seymour. "Someone must eat the cakes we have prepared."

When they entered the cottage, Charlotte noticed the paint spill had been expertly cleaned up by Ella so that not a trace of the colour or broken glass remained. Mrs. Seymour went straight to the seat beside the teapot and said, "Do have a seat, Mr. Collins, wherever you like. We must forgo the usual polite formalities. The water is getting cold."

Indeed, a different atmosphere pervaded the room than what had been there a half an hour before. Mr. Collins seemed to be so like them in taste and sensibility that Mrs. Seymour felt she was entertaining a young nephew, and not a stranger. Charlotte, for her part, did not know what she felt. Dressed in her widow's garment, she had no illusions about her appearance. She believed that black, combined with the simplicity of her gown and the styling of her hair, made her look much older than her years. Yet there were moments, during a lull in the conversation, when Mr. Collins would turn to look at her, and she thought she saw, in his eyes, a look that held something more than polite attention.

There was a slight crisis when Mr. Collins revealed, after noting a volume of poetry sitting on a nearby table, that he was fond of verse, too.

"Who are your favorite poets, Mr. Collins? You admire Shakespeare and Milton, I presume?" Charlotte asked. She knew their guest had fallen in Mrs. Seymour's esteem, but he could regain his position by professing a regard for those two giants of English literature, who occupied such a lofty place that even Mrs. Seymour could not deny their greatness.

"I suppose one cannot claim to admire poetry without admiring those two," he replied. "Although to be perfectly frank, I find them too distant for my taste. I much prefer Thomas Gray. He speaks in a language I can understand and inspires me to record the musings of my own wanderings through the country churchyards of life."

"Then you write verse, as well as read it?" Mrs. Seymour asked, with narrowing eyes.

"Yes, I confess to the crime," he replied with a smile. "And by your looks, Mrs. Seymour, I see that in your eyes it is a heinous deed. But I assure you I am no Lord Byron, even though I have scribbled an ode or two. I am too far below the notice of society to try to scandalize it with either my behavior or my prosody."

"Perhaps today you are unknown," said Charlotte. "But when your poems are published …"

"That they shall never be, Lady Ashe. My poems are for my eyes only. They are my companions on lonely nights when I … Forgive me. I wander into paths I would prefer to avoid when in such pleasant company. May I have another one of these scones? They are delicious."

"Of course," said Charlotte, handing him the plate.

"This cottage is very snug," Mr. Collins said, after Charlotte had also passed him the butter. "Sitting by the fire in a cozy room, drinking tea and eating scones, it all reminds me of my childhood home in Whitby."

"Whitby!" Mrs. Seymour exclaimed. "Are you from Whitby, Mr. Collins?"

"Yes. Do you know it?"

"Know it? I spent two of the happiest years of my life in Whitby. I moved there right after I married my first husband. Mr. George. He was a lieutenant in the King's navy. His ship went down in the winter of 1773."

"I am sorry to hear it, Ma'am."

"It happened a very long time ago, Mr. Collins. And later I had the good fortune to marry Mr. Seymour, even though I was a widow without a fortune. So I suppose I really must not complain. But I do have such fond memories of Whitby. There is nothing to compare to one's first love, when one is young and full of optimism and ..." Mrs. Seymour stopped in mid-sentence, suddenly aware that in her enthusiasm for the past she had tumbled into subjects that were painful for the two young people seated at the table.

"I am traveling to Whitby next week," said Mr. Collins, bringing to an end the awkward silence that had ensued. "Perhaps you and Lady Ashe would join me."

Before Mrs. Seymour could reply, Charlotte said, "That is very kind of you, but I presume you intended to travel by horseback. We should not wish to disrupt your plans."

"I do not mind traveling by carriage. If it is the extra horses that concern you, the company of you and Mrs. Seymour would more than repay me for the expense."

"We could make an outing out of it," said Mrs. Seymour. "Ella could prepare a picnic basket. And you, Charlotte, could take your sketching pad."

"Then it is decided," said Mr. Collins.

Mrs. Seymour, her eyes now sparkling with goodwill, nodded toward the gentleman's empty plate and said, "Do try the sponge cake, Mr. Collins."

VIII.

The morning air was still fresh when they set out for Whitby. Although Charlotte was determined to broach the topic of her husband and his gambling debts during their outing, and not let the opportunity slip away as she had done during their meeting at the cottage, there never seemed to be an appropriate time to do so. Mrs. Seymour, who was in excellent spirits, glanced out the window at regular intervals, and each time she did so she remarked upon the reviving qualities of a carriage ride in the countryside, thereby keeping the conversation centered on polite nothings about the benefits of country air and sunlight. When that topic was temporarily exhausted, Mr. Collins entertained the two ladies by telling them stories about the country homes they passed, displaying an impressive knowledge of the history of the moors. And so almost before they knew it they caught their first glimpse of the sea, first just a ribbon of deep blue, and even Charlotte joined with Mrs. Seymour in expressing a small cry of delight at the sight.

After the carriage was stabled at a Whitby inn, Mr. Collins went to attend to the business that had brought him to the sea-faring town. Charlotte and Mrs. Seymour were therefore left to stroll through the busy streets, until the agreed upon hour when they would all meet at the old Abbey that stood atop the harbour's East Cliff.

Their progress was slow, since Mrs. Seymour had an intense interest in every shop window they passed. But Charlotte did not mind. She, too, felt the reviving qualities of a change of scenery. Her only sorrow was that she could not make a present of the new bonnet her aunt was so admiring. However, the bonnet was soon forgotten in the happy chance meeting of an old friend.

"Mrs. Williams, is it really you?" Mrs. Seymour exclaimed.

"Beneath the wrinkles it is the same face I wore when we were young," the cheerful woman replied. "But what are we doing standing and talking in the road, when I have a kettle at home waiting to be set upon the fire?"

Mrs. Williams led them up a steep lane, until they reached a narrow house that stood on such an incline that it looked ready to topple down to the harbour at any moment. "It takes some getting used to," Mrs. Williams explained, pointing out the sloping door frames and window casements. "Yet though the house may slope the roof does not leak, which is a blessing, as Mr. Williams so often reminds me."

"And you have a lovely view of the harbour," said Charlotte, who was immediately attracted to the window that looked out to the sea. "Do you mind if I sketch it?"

Mrs. Williams did not mind at all, since with Charlotte so employed she and Mrs. Seymour could have a nice gossip at their leisure. Charlotte was still engaged with sketching the sails of the lone fishing boat that sat perched just beyond the shelter of the cliff when the clock struck the hour and Mrs. Williams exclaimed, "Has the time gone as quickly as that? I must deliver these food baskets to the poor, before Mr. Williams returns for his dinner. Will you be joining us, my dears? There is nothing as tasty as a fish pulled fresh out of these waters."

"We must decline," Mrs. Seymour replied. "We are picnicking on the Abbey grounds with our neighbour, Mr. John Collins. He is Whitby born and raised. Do you know the family?"

"Collins is a common enough name," replied Mrs. Seymour, "as is John. Although I cannot say I remember such a man."

"He would be of the same age as my niece, Lady Ashe."

"No, I cannot say I am remembering him. Perhaps Mr. Williams would have a better recollection."

Before they parted, Mrs. Williams directed the two ladies to the one hundred and ninety-nine steps that led up to the Abbey. Charlotte was concerned the steep climb might be too much for her aunt, since Mrs. Seymour was not used to taking much exercise. However, the combination of being in Whitby and meeting an old friend had restored much of her youthful energy and so the two ladies reached the top of the hill only slightly out of breath. After a few minutes rest at a stone bench that sat outside the St. Mary's churchyard, they continued on to the Abbey.

"It is magnificent!" Charlotte exclaimed, as they approached the ruins of the ancient, once venerable structure.

"I am surprised neither your grandfather nor I ever thought to bring you here," said Mrs. Seymour. "There are so many interesting views to sketch. I suppose your grandfather felt Whitby did not have enough polish for an heiress."

"Well, I am no longer an heiress and so I may now enjoy Whitby as I please. Shall we take a walk around?"

Only the stone shell remained of the Gothic-style Norman Abbey, which dated back to the thirteenth and fourteenth centuries — and nothing remained of the Anglo-Saxon monastery built in the 600s, which had been ruled by a formidable royal princess named Abbess Hild. The older monastery had been laid waste by the Danes in the ninth century, while the monastery built on its ruins was partially destroyed by King Henry VIII during his Dissolution of the Monasteries, a part of that monarch's scheme to separate England from papal authority. Yet even though the wind swept through the tall casements that once housed brightly coloured windows, and the stone floor that had once traversed the long nave had long since been covered over with grass, neither time nor war could totally erase the sense of awe that still permeated the once sacred space. And so Charlotte wandered through the roofless ruin, at times allowing her gaze to follow the triple-tiered stone columns that led upward toward heaven, at times peering through a graceful portal whose view led to the sea below, and at all times filled with admiration.

When they finished their tour of the inside, they strolled around the ruin's outer perimeter. They went as far as a pond, where a few ducks were lazily swimming. From that vantage point there was a view of the Abbey that looked from the north facade down to where the apse had once stood. Charlotte took out her pencils and sketching pad and Mrs. Seymour took out a novel by Mrs. Fanny Burney. They were therefore both happily employed when Mr. Collins joined them.

"You have chosen a charming spot, Lady Ashe," he said. "It affords an excellent view of the Abbey."

"I am afraid I have been overly ambitious. I cannot get right the perspective."

"The Abbey does not reveal all her mysteries on a first meeting." He then turned to Mrs. Seymour and said, "Shall we have our picnic here, or do you prefer another spot?"

"I am quite comfortable," she replied, "and it would be cruel to deny the ducks their pleasure. They have been eyeing our basket for some time."

And so they spread their cloth and took out the good food Ella had packed for them and remarked on the warmness of the sun and the pleasant music made by the gulls flying overhead. When Mrs. Seymour's eyelids began to droop, Charlotte took the opportunity to remark, "I believe there is a poet associated with the Abbey's history. Do you know of him, Mr. Collins?"

"You are referring to Caedmon. He lived during the days of the Abbess Hild. If the story written by the Venerable Bede is true, he was a simple herdsman who worked for the Abbey. At supper, the workers would entertain themselves by playing upon the harp and singing. But when the harp was passed to him, Caedmon was silent. He thought he had no poetry within him."

"How sad."

"It is true of many people, I have found."

"How did he discover he was a poet?"

"It seems one night he fell asleep and in his dream a mysterious man came to him and asked him to sing. 'I cannot sing to other men,' Caedmon told his nocturnal visitor. 'Then sing to *me*,' said the man. 'I do not know what to sing about,' Caedmon protested. '*I* will tell you what to sing,' said the man. 'Sing about the Creation of all things.' And so in his dream Caedmon began to sing. And when he awoke his song was still with him. He sang his poem for the Abbess, who recognized its genius. Caedmon was then taken from the animal pens and given a place at the monks' table. From that day he was given new work — to compose more poetry. And it seems everything he wrote was sublime."

"What a wonderful story! Do you think it is true?"

"I like to think so. The Abbess Hild must have been a remarkable woman."

"Why do you say that?"

"Not every woman can look past a man's rough clothes and manners and see the poetry inside him."

Charlotte could feel a blush begin to steal across her cheeks. She therefore turned her head and threw a few crusts of bread to the ducks that had waddled close to where they were sitting, before asking, "Did any of his poems survive?"

"Bede quotes a fragment."

"Can you say it?"

"Not the Anglo-Saxon. But I do remember a phrase, in English, that I learned in school: *'He first created for the sons of men Heaven as a roof.'* I thought about those words a great deal when I was in Spain, where we often had to sleep out in the field, and how it was a kindness of God to create a roof for His creatures. When a person has a roof over his head, he does not feel so defenseless and alone." He then added, "I suppose you have heard the gossip, that I was Lord Ashe's valet in Spain."

Charlotte, who had been taken by surprise by this sudden mention of her husband, could think of no other reply, except to say, "I did hear it spoken of."

"My family was in trade, not in service. But I was a young man desperate to see the world. I would have slept with the animals, like Caedmon, if that is where the recruiting officer had sent me. When Lord Ashe's first valet was seriously wounded, I was promoted from the ranks of the regular soldiers to take the man's place. I was quite fond of Lord Ashe, if a former valet can say such words without giving offense. He was very kind to me, and I was greatly saddened when I learned of his death. I've written a poem for him, a kind of elegy, but I do not suppose you would care to hear it."

"I would very much like to hear it, Mr. Collins."

"I am afraid it is not very good."

"I showed you my sketch of the Abbey."

"That is true. Well, then ..." He removed a piece of paper from his coat pocket and carefully unfolded it. "It is called 'Ode to a Dead Lord.' I have written just the first two stanzas."

He gave Charlotte one more look, as though to say, *You still have a chance to stop me.* When she returned his look with a smile of encouragement, he began to read:

Bright star, that glitters in the night,
Silent, old, and, lonely;
Do you glance down upon this pitiable sight,
A world grown cold and contumely?
Do you hear the young widow's sigh,
The groan of the old man worn out from labour;
Does your heart break at the innocent babe's cry,
The last sob of the young lord, fallen from Fortune's
favour?

Bright star, the ages pass by
Each one in their season;
The king spinning his plot, the fisherman setting his net,
Are they all one to your stony-eyed reason?
Do you laugh at the lover who cannot forget,
The wounded soldier all bloody and pale;
And jeer at one who remembers with a sigh,
A young lord, his left hand raised in farewell?

When he came to the end, both he and Charlotte were silent. Then he said, "It pained me very much to see what happened to Lord Ashe after the Campaign, when we were back in England. I tried to help him. I had made my fortune on the Stock Exchange — it was more luck than good sense that led me to invest in the right shares — and had I not been married I would have given him every last shilling in my pocket. I would have done anything to stop him from taking his own life."

Charlotte looked at him. "You believe it was suicide, Mr. Collins?"

"What else could it have been?"

"Murder."

"That is a serious accusation, Lady Ashe. Have you a reason?"

"It is more a feeling than a fact I can point to. Unless—"

"Unless?"

"There was something strange about that room. I mentioned to Mr. Bryght—"

"Mr. Bryght?"

"Mr. Theo Bryght is a Bow Street Runner from London who is investigating my husband's death. It is very likely he will make an attempt to speak with you."

"I am at his service, should he require my assistance."

"I was sure you would be willing to help."

"But you were saying something about the room."

"Yes, I told Mr. Bryght that I thought a piece of blotting paper was missing from Lord Ashe's writing box. That might suggest my husband was writing a letter when the murderer entered the room, and the murderer took both the letter and the blotting paper."

"Why would someone do such a thing?"

"If the letter had in it something about the murderer, or the reason for their quarrel, the murderer would wish to destroy the evidence."

"You have given the matter much thought."

"I did think I was being very clever. But your poem has reminded me that I have missed the point entirely."

"My poem?"

"Yes, when you mention Lord Ashe raising his left hand in farewell. You would know he was left-handed, having been his valet."

"And so?"

"My husband's right hand had been slit by a pen knife, according to Mr. Bryght."

"That would make sense. He would have used his left hand to grasp the knife."

"But if the knife was in his left hand, why did the constable find it lying beside my husband's right foot? Would it not be more likely that it would have either fallen on to the table or on the floor beside my husband's left foot?"

"I do not have an answer. I have no experience in such matters." He then added, "Do you have a suspicion as to who murdered your husband?"

Charlotte knew this was the opportunity she had been waiting for. But instead of speaking about her husband's debts, very different words flew out of her mouth, words that had neither her consent nor her control.

"Mr. Collins, were you truly fond of Lord Ashe?" she asked. "You are not saying it only because I am his widow and so you do not wish to offend my feelings?"

"I would have taken your feelings into consideration, Lady Ashe, if my sentiments had not been genuine. But I had no reason to lie, on your account."

"And were you a close friend of Lord Ashe?"

"I was a loyal friend. I did not forget the difference in rank that stood between us."

"But you knew who his friends were?"

"Yes."

"And if Lord Ashe would have had a mistress, you would have known that, as well?"

Mr. Collins turned away his eyes. "Forgive me, but I am not accustomed to speak of such matters with a lady."

"What colour was her hair? Was she fair or dark?"

"Lady Ashe, you must stop tormenting yourself."

"Did she love him very much?"

Mr. Collins stood and, turning toward the town, said, "We must be on our way, if we wish to be in Butterhill before dark. I shall go ahead to the inn and see to the horses."

"Mr. Collins," she said, following after him, "you are the only person in the world I can ask. You are the only person who knows the truth. Who was she? I must know."

"I cannot reveal the lady's name without destroying her honour — and mine."

IX.

When they returned to the cottage, Mrs. Seymour retired to her room, happy but exhausted from the day's journey. Charlotte was glad of the quiet. She needed to sort through her troubling thoughts.

She could not think back to her interview with Mr. Collins without embarrassment. Even she had not realized the depth of her anguish until the moment when she had pressed the man to reveal the name of her husband's mistress. Yet why did she care so much? Had she been so naive to think her husband would remain chaste after their separation?

She was not a schoolgirl, an eternal "Miss" stubbornly locking herself inside the nursery, she decided. She had known, somewhere in a dark corner of her troubled heart, there would be others. A gentleman's primary occupation in life was to be amused. Hunting, and gambling, and dining were all enlisted in the daily fight against the dreaded disease of boredom. Flirting and making love were weapons in the arsenal, too.

But why had he kept the locket, and the lock of hair? And why had she revealed so much to Mr. Collins, a man she hardly knew — and whom it was more fitting for her to despise?

A flush of crimson stole across her cheek. "You must not fall in love with him," she whispered through clenched teeth.

CANTO THE THIRD

Theo Bryght glanced in the direction of the horizon. A thick blanket of clouds had rolled in, as was usual at the end of the day, turning the sea into a muddy swirl, which beckoned to him more forcefully than sparkling blue waters. And so even though his intention had been to get a late afternoon repast at some inn, he instead clambered down onto the sand and found a place to sit.

The solemn rhythm of the returning waves making their daily futile assault against the pebbly beach was a perfect accompaniment for his thoughts. He was not happy. He was not happy with Lord Ashe, he was not happy with Brighton, and he was not happy with himself. By now he should have either found the murderer or proven the death had been by suicide. Yet the truth remained as elusive as ever.

His visits to some of Lord Ashe's supposedly closest friends had proved to be spectacularly unproductive. Lord Jones-Bryce, a small man with a large fortune, whose perpetually red face had earned him the nickname of Carrot Nose, could only say Lord Ashe was "a splendid fellow." When asked if he could recall his whereabouts on the night of the murder, the eyes of the red-faced lord had grown wide, as though the thought of being able to recall, in the morning, where one drank and gambled away the night was a novel one.

An interview with another friend, the Honourable Simon Stopehill, had revealed the fact that Lord Ashe was "a real out and outer," but nothing else. Lady Cecily Molebarrow, who assured Theo Bryght she had been one of Lord Ashe's dearest friends, could reveal nothing about the young lord's affairs, whether of the pocketbook or the heart. A young man named Martinson, whom Theo Bryght had tracked down in a boxing club, had tried to convince the Runner that he and Lord Ashe had not been such good friends as people has supposed, since Ashe was often too short of blunt to be amusing. Theo Bryght had then tried to track down another gentleman, a Lord Lauferby, but the young man never seemed to be where he should be. When the Runner called at Lauferby's home, the butler informed him the young gentleman was at his tailor. When he paid a visit to the tailor's shop, the young man had just left.

One theory could be discarded, however. Lord Ashe's death could not have been caused by a tradesman going berserk. If that had been the case, the streets of Brighton would have been littered with the corpses of the English aristocracy. There was not a shopkeeper in Brighton who did not have his stack of unpaid and overdue bills, Theo Bryght had found out. Yet the merchants were, on the whole, a singularly cheerful lot. Perhaps they had been permanently affected by the perpetual gaiety of the place.

To make matters worse, with each passing day the scent was growing colder. By the following week the murder would be totally forgotten, if Theo Bryght knew Brighton — and he was confident he did. He had learned that Prinny was due to arrive in Brighton the following week, and once the Prince Regent was in town the Beau

Monde would be busy with their parties and their clothes and their new topics of gossip. No one would have the time or inclination to discuss the murder of a mere viscount, not even one who had been a "splendid fellow" and a "real out and outer."

"Hello, I thought that was you. I am Lord Lauferby. I heard you wished to speak with me."

Theo Bryght looked up. Standing to the side of him was a young man wearing tan pantaloons, a mauve frockcoat, and a lemon-coloured waistcoat that was topped by a tall and highly starched cravat. *A regular tulip*, Theo Bryght decided. If the young man's foppish dress was an indication, it was doubtful Lord Lauferby would have anything useful to say. On the other hand, one never knew who had the piece of information that would unlock the mystery, and so the Runner said, "Yes, I do have a few questions I would like to ask you."

Lord Lauferby had no great desire to soil his elegant clothes. But when he saw the Runner had no intention of rising from his seat, he gingerly lifted the hem of his coat and sat down on the sand. "A grisly business," he said, wiping clean the tops of his highly polished boots with a handkerchief. "One hears of such things happening among the poorer classes, of course. But Ashe was one of us! Of course, he was several years younger than you, so you might not have known him."

Theo Bryght shot a look over at his companion. "Why should I have known him?"

"It is no use shamming it any longer. Smythe recognized you, when you were nosing around the gambling club. That is the trouble with very old servants. They remember too much. He recognized you at once."

"And ran to tell you of his discovery? That does not sound like Smythe."

"No, Smythe knows his place. But he was unsure how to address you, in the future, and so he asked me for advice — confidentially, you understand — since he did not wish to be disrespectful. And I am sure you can sympathize with the old man's predicament. It is Nathaniel Clermont, the younger son of the fifth Earl of Warrington, to whom I am speaking, is it not?"

Theo Bryght gave a slight bow.

"Smythe remembered that your father and my father had been great friends, when they were young. Although it is hard to think of one's parents as ever being young, I suppose Smythe's memory is correct."

Lord Lauferby shooed away a gull that had joined them in their conversation. Then he added, "Smythe assured me he is not in the least bit curious to know why the son of an Earl is pretending to be a Bow Street Runner. 'It is not my place to be curious about the doings of the gentry, Lord Lauferby,' he told me. I, however, being a member of the gentry do not mind admitting I am interested. If I am going to be questioned about a murder, I do want to know who is doing the questioning, you understand."

Theo Bryght did. Although he had no wish to divulge the details of his past, he knew Lord Lauferby had a legitimate claim to the information. One had a duty to answer the questions of a Bow Street Runner, whereas one could remain silent when asked those same questions by an idle member of the aristocracy.

"My father insisted I become a clergyman," he therefore told Lord Lauferby. "A good living was available on our family estate, complete with a luxurious house. I had his permission to hire a curate to perform the more tiresome duties, which would leave me free to occupy my time as I wished. And so in my father's eyes there was no earthly reason why I should refuse such a generous offer."

"Yet you did?"

"Yes."

"Why?"

"I knew in my heart I was not a clergyman."

"You gave up a good livelihood because of that?" Lord Lauferby asked with amazement.

"Perhaps in the eyes of the society we were born into it was a foolish reason. But I felt I could not live my entire life in a lie. And so I gave it all up. Or, rather, my father tried the old trick of threatening to disinherit me — and when he discovered that I refused to budge from my position he made good on his promise. I rather foolishly assumed that with time my father would relent and give me a living in some other manner. But he fell off a horse and broke his neck before the touching reconciliation could take place. My brother, the present Earl of Warrington, and I had never gotten along, and so he was only too happy to keep things as they were."

"It defies belief," said the young lord, shaking his head. "How did you live without having any blunt in your pocket?"

"It was hard, at first. I will admit to that. There were many times when I uttered a prayer my brother would follow the example of our father and break his neck, as well — which was further proof, in my opinion, that I was eminently unsuitable for a religious calling. But since my brother did not oblige, and his wife began to present him with a brood of sons to take his place, should the untimely event ever occur, I slowly became resigned to my lot in life and looked about for some work I might be good at. It took time, not having done much work before, but in the end I found it, in Bow Street."

"Are you good at it? Do you think you will discover the cause of Ashe's death?"

"Would that worry you, if I did?"

Lord Lauferby tried to laugh, but the sound that came out of his mouth had a hollow ring to it. "Why should I worry? Ashe was a friend."

"But you are worried. I can see it, and I imagine that is why you have been avoiding me. Yet there is something you would like to tell me, is there not?"

When the young lord remained silent, Theo Bryght tried to make it easier for him by saying, "Tell me what happened on the day of the murder. Did you see Lord Ashe in the afternoon?"

"No. I went riding in the afternoon. I had asked Ashe to come to my rooms for dinner. I had invited a few other friends."

"A gentlemen's party?"

"Yes, you could call it that."

"What time did your guests arrive?"

"Between 7:30 and 8:00."

"Was Lord March a member of the party?"

"Good lord, no! He is even older than you are!"

"And as dull?"

"Really, Clermont—"

"My name is Bryght, now. Theo Bryght. Please remember that."

"Very well, Bryght, and you surely remember how young men are. There is a world of difference between a man of twenty-five and thirty-five."

"I will accept that. So there was you, and Lord Ashe, and who else? Was Mr. John Collins invited to your party?"

Lord Lauferby shifted uncomfortably in his pebbly seat. "He might have been."

"It is a yes or no question, Lord Lauferby."

The young man pursed his lips. Apparently, the memory of inviting a former valet to a dinner party still left an unpleasant taste in his mouth. With great effort he finally blurted out, "What else can a person do when he is on the rocks?"

"So John Collins was also there. Was Mr. Collins paying the debts of all of your party?"

"No. Carrot Nose — that is, Lord Jones-Bryce — is full of juice, so he can afford to be a high-flyer. The same goes for Martinson and Stopehill. They are always fairly flush in the pockets, even though they are younger sons. It was just Lord Ashe and I who were short of blunt."

"Had you received money from Collins before?"

"No. He was Ashe's Gull-groper. But I was in pretty deep, thanks to some ivory tuners at a gaming hell in … Well, it does not matter where, does it?"

Theo Bryght shook his head. One gambling den was the same as another, in his experience. Although everyone knew cheating was rampant in such places, for some reason young men of the upper classes, buoyed by a large amount of drink, thought they would be able to beat the odds and emerge a winner. And so the Runner said, "No, it does not matter. But you were pretty deep in debt, you say?"

"And so I asked Ashe if he thought Collins might be able to lend me some gingerbread, too."

"What was Lord Ashe's reply?"

"Between you and me, Bryght, I do not think Ashe was happy with the idea. Probably worried Collins would run out of the dibs. But there was one debt in particular I needed to pay back before the end of the month and so I insisted until Ashe finally agreed to bring along Collins."

"Did you broach the subject to Mr. Collins at your dinner party?"

"Yes. Or at least I think so. We were all fairly foxed by the time we finished dining. And then we all went to the gaming club, where we had even more to drink."

"If you had money to gamble, you must have gotten it from somewhere."

"That is what makes the whole thing so befogged. I have a recollection Collins gave me some blunt, and I gave him my vowels. But when I woke up the next morning, the vowels were in my purse."

"Perhaps you won at the gaming table and were able to repay Mr. Collins."

"I should remember winning, I would think."

Theo Bryght tried not to smile. He was not so old that he did not remember being infatuated with cards and drink, despite the fact it was a one-sided *tendre* since he rarely won. Yet he also had pity for the young lord. Lord Lauferby's youth gave him a certain a charm, but in twenty years he would most likely be fat and purple in the face, his health and intellect destroyed by too much drink and frivolous living.

"Let us go back to the dinner party," said the Runner, returning his thoughts to the business at hand. "Did Lord Ashe look worried, or seem to be distracted?"

"Not more than usual."

"So he was worried about something?"

"Other than money, you mean to say?"

"You must tell me. I did not know Lord Ashe."

"He changed after he married."

"People often do."

"The marriage was not a success. I suppose you have heard about that."

"I have heard Lord Ashe gambled away the lady's fortune."

"That was what I found so strange. We all get cucumberish from time to time. But I never knew Ashe to gamble so heavily before he was married."

"Perhaps he never before had the chance to do so. I believe the lady came with fifty thousand pounds."

Lord Lauferby shook his head. "He married for money, there is no denying that. But I do not believe he married to waste it. Something happened to him, later."

"Did Lord Ashe have a mistress?"

"I do not know."

Theo Bryght raised an eyebrow. Men usually were not shy about discussing their conquests.

Lord Lauferby acknowledged the hint and said, "I am telling you the truth. The way he always avoided the subject was too smoky by half."

By this time the sun had set and Theo Bryght felt the chill in the air. He would eat an early dinner, he decided, preferably one served next to a blazing fire. Yet he was reluctant to bring the interview to a close without gleaning at least one new fact or a new lead, and so he asked, "Why did Lord Ashe need such large sums of money?"

"To pay his debts of honour."

"But why did he gamble for such large stakes in the first place? There are gentlemen who know their limit and can walk away from the gaming table when their losses are too high. Carrot Nose drinks and gambles, yet he has never gone so far as to lose his family estate at cards. I assume you, Lord Lauferby, are able to exhibit a similar prudence. Why was Ashe different? What happened to him?"

"I do not know," Lord Lauferby replied, "unless it had something to do with this." The young lord removed a crumpled piece of paper from his pocket and showed it to the Runner.

Theo Bryght read what was written on the page. There was just one word: Spain.

"What does it mean?" the Runner asked.

"I have no idea."

"The letter is not franked," said Theo Bryght, turning the page in his hands.

"No, it was delivered to my rooms by a messenger. My butler could not remember more, except that it was a young boy, the kind one always sees on the street. You do not think, do you, someone wishes to blackmail me?"

"I have no idea. Did you do something in Spain that would warrant being blackmailed?"

"Not that I can remember."

"Then you have nothing to worry about."

"Perhaps that is what Ashe thought, too."

II.

After finishing his dinner, Theo Bryght returned to the gaming club where, presumably, Lord Ashe had gambled away his wife's estate. The hour was still early — the fashionable world would not start arriving until closer to midnight — and so he correctly assumed he could ask a few more questions without annoying Smythe. Now that he had a little more information, he hoped Smythe might be more forthcoming.

"And please do me the favour of calling me Mr. Bryght," he said to the elderly servant, after allowing Smythe to escort him into the main gaming room.

"Yes, sir," replied Smythe, pleased to be in on the secret. "Would you like a glass of wine, Mr. Bryght? If I remember correctly —"

"You are to remember nothing about my preferences in wine or anything else, Smythe. Remember, you never saw me before this nasty business concerning Lord Ashe's death."

"Very good, sir. How may I be of service, if I may ask?"

Theo Bryght glanced about the large room. The chairs were all neatly arranged around the gaming tables. There was an air of unreality about the place, and he imagined this must be how a theatre felt, before the performance began.

"Tell me again, Smythe, where was Lord Ashe sitting?"

"I do not believe I told you that information, sir. There are so many gentlemen it is hard to remember who was sitting where. I cannot even say for sure that Lord Ashe was here that evening."

"I believe Lord Lauferby was a member of Lord Ashe's party. Does that help you remember?"

Theo Bryght noted with satisfaction that Smythe was wiping his hands on his apron, a sure sign the elderly servant was agitated — and that his question had hit its mark.

"Lord Lauferby, sir?"

"Yes, I spoke with Lord Lauferby this afternoon and he mentioned that the two of them arrived together. They were good friends, as everyone knows. I would suppose, then, they often sat together at the same gaming table. And gentlemen often have a favorite table, a table they return to whenever they are here. Is that not true?"

"Yes, sir, there are gentlemen like that."

"So it would be quite within reason for an old servant like you to recall where a certain gentleman sat, if it was his regular place. It would not be like divulging a secret, at all."

Theo Bryght waited for his words to sink in. He did not fault Smythe for his hesitance to reveal what he knew. Any good servant would do the same. But he did want to move forward with his inquiry. Someone had to begin to talk.

"I believe they usually sat in the back, sir. That table under the chandelier."

"Who else was sitting with them at the table on the night Lord Ashe died?"

"I am sorry, but I cannot recall who else was there. You see, I did not know at the time the night would be of such importance."

"Yet you do recall that Lord Lauferby and Lord Ashe were there?"

Smythe assumed the air of a man who had a secret, but wanted some coaxing before he would reveal it.

"If it is gossip getting about that worries you, I am no longer a member of the Beau Monde," Theo Bryght reminded him. "What you tell me will remain confidential."

"Lord Lauferby was found under the table the following morning. He was still feeling the effect of .... ahem ...The wine here is of a very good quality, sir, very powerful."

"I understand. Under the table, you say?"

"Yes, sir."

"One would remember that."

"Yes, sir."

"So you did not see Lord Ashe and Lord Lauferby leave together?"

"How could they, sir, if Lord Lauferby spent the night here?"

"Perhaps the two left at some point during the evening, and then Lord Lauferby returned alone?"

"That is possible."

"Smythe, please think carefully. Lord Ashe did leave this place alive. That is no secret. If he had not, you would have discovered his body, as well. So did you see him leave? Did you see who he left with?"

"I am sorry, sir, but I am afraid I cannot help you. I have many duties, and staff not being what they used to be, I also have many cares.

"Is there anyone who might have seen Lord Ashe leave?"

"You already asked that question of the staff, sir. I would rather not get them all stirred up again."

"I understand. Thank you, Smythe."

"Thank you, sir."

Theo Bryght turned to leave. Then he stopped and asked one last question.

"Smythe, who found Lord Lauferby's body?"

"Beg your pardon, sir?"

"You said Lord Lauferby was discovered in the morning, under the table. Who found him?"

"I did, sir."

"No one else?"

"No, sir."

After Theo Bryght left the room, Smythe returned to his many duties. But as he walked down the hall toward the kitchen, a boy sprang in front of him.

"Mr. Smythe, why didn't you let me talk to that Runner?"

"This is no matter for children, Tom. If you know what's good for you, you'll let me do the talking for you."

"But I was the one who found Lord Lauferby under that table."

"And the sooner you forget about that unfortunate incident, the better. Now run along and have your supper."

III.

The next morning Theo Bryght returned to Mrs. Barker's lodging house. The proprietress greeted him with the same sour face as on his previous visits.

"I cannot think what more there is for you to see in that room, Mr. Bryght."

"Nevertheless, see it again I must. And please send up that girl of yours. Rosemary is her name, I believe."

Mr. Bryght strode up the stairs, without waiting for a reply. In truth, he did not blame Mrs. Barker for her impatience to be done with him. In her place, he would have felt the same, he supposed. But Lord Lauferby's one-word letter had cast a new light upon the case. If blackmail was involved, perhaps Lady Ashe had been right about the missing blotting paper. Perhaps Lord Ashe had been in the middle of writing a letter when he was interrupted by the blackmailer. And perhaps one of the blackmailer's notes, if there had been notes, had survived.

The room had been emptied of Lord Ashe's possessions, but there were still much for the Runner to do. First he checked the fireplace, which had not been used since the night of the young man's death. He rummaged through the ashes, hoping to find the remains of a letter that had been tossed into the fire, but his efforts were not rewarded with success.

Next he checked the table where Lord Ashe had been sitting. Perhaps he had missed a secret drawer. But he had not. Still sitting on the table was a small stack of letters and invitations. He had already been through them, which is how he discovered the names of Lord Ashe's friends. He glanced through them again, hoping that something of a more sinister nature might come to light, now there was a possibility of blackmail. But another reading proved to be a waste of his time.

By that time, though, there was a knock at the door. He turned around and said, "Hello. You are Rosemary, are you not?"

"Yes, sir," said the girl, who remained standing by the door.

"It is not pleasant being in a room where a dead person was found, is it?"

"No, sir."

"But I suppose you will have to come inside the room some day. Once the inquiry is over, Mrs. Barker will let the room to someone else. You will have to make the fire and bring in the tea. Is that not so?"

"I suppose so, sir."

Since she was still reluctant to enter the room, he did not continue to press the issue. Instead, he went to the door and said, "Rosemary, it is very important you tell me everything you know. Do you understand?"

The girl nodded, but it was not a convincing nod. Theo Bryght was sure Mrs. Barker had instructed her to say nothing more than the basic facts. Somehow he had to impress upon the girl that she had more to gain by trusting him than she had to fear from Mrs. Barker. Since she was a pretty girl, he was almost certain of the tact to take.

"Lord Ashe was a nice gentleman, I understand."

"Oh, yes, sir," she replied, brightening up.

"If he had needed your help while he was alive, I imagine you would have helped him."

"Yes, sir."

"Well, even though he is dead, he still needs our help. You see, people are saying he took his own life. We must clear his name, Rosemary. It is up to you and me to do it. I will therefore ask you a few more questions, and this time you must tell me everything you know. For Lord Ashe's sake, you understand?"

"Yes, sir. I'll try."

"When was the last time you saw Lord Ashe alive?"

"I don't know, sir."

Theo Bryght successfully suppressed a groan. It would not do to show his disappointment that his efforts to win her confidence had failed at the crucial moment. He therefore assumed a kind expression and said, "He had a dinner engagement at around eight. Did you see him before that? Perhaps he rang for some hot water, or a brush, or a cup of tea?"

"A brush! Yes, sir. I brought him up a brush at about seven o'clock. The clock at the top of the landing was chiming, which is how I know the time. How clever of you to know about the brush!"

He smiled. Apparently, the girl thought a Bow Street Runner never had a need to brush down his coat before going to dinner.

"And so you brought Lord Ashe a brush. Do you remember what he was doing when you entered the room?"

When the girl's only reply were the blushes that covered her face, he continued, saying, "I would suppose, since Lord Ashe was dressing for a dinner party, he might have been in the middle of tying his cravat. And I further suppose, since Lord Ashe did not have a man to help him, that he might have asked you, Rosemary, to assist him."

Since the girl's blushes had become even brighter, Theo Bryght knew he was on the right track. He therefore continued, saying, "And gentlemen being what they are, it is not unlikely to suppose that while your hands were occupied with tying the cravat that Lord Ashe's hands were occupied about your waist. And so we may assume, may we not, Rosemary, that Lord Ashe was very much alive at seven o'clock?"

"Yes, sir," she managed to stammer. Then she added, "Please, sir, you won't tell Mrs. Barker?"

"No, Rosemary. It will be our secret."

"Thank you, sir."

"I assume Lord Ashe was in a cheerful mood. Is that correct, Rosemary?" When he saw the girl did not immediately rep, he asked, "Did he appear to be worried about something?"

"I cannot say for sure, Mr. Bryght."

"But there was something …?"

The girl began to blush again, which made Theo Bryght begin to wish the girl was not so "Miss-ish." But since he could not change her nature, he carried on with his inquiry, saying, "What made you think Lord Ashe was worried? Remember, Rosemary, I need your help."

"Well, you see, sir, usually when Lord Ashe would put his arms around me, he would try to kiss me, too."

"But he did not that night?"

"No, sir. He gave me a little squeeze, but I think what he wanted, really, was help with the cravat. He looked very pale, and I told him that perhaps he should not go out if he was ill."

"What did he say to that?"

"He said he was just a little under the weather, but he would be fine once he had a good dinner in him."

"And was he better, when he returned to his rooms?"

"I wouldn't know, sir. He usually returned very late, after I was already in bed."

"He had his own latchkey?"

"Yes, sir."

"And so you do not know if he returned alone, or if he was accompanied by another gentleman?"

"No, sir."

"You did not hear any voices, later? Perhaps you were awakened in the middle of the night? The sound of two men quarreling might do that."

"No, sir. I did not hear a thing. I am a sound sleeper. Cook says it would take an earthquake to wake me up."

"Did Cook hear anything? She might have mentioned something to you in the kitchen."

"No, sir. Cook did not hear anything."

Theo Bryght was not entirely convinced. But he did not expect the girl to tell tales about her superior, just as he did not expect the cook to tell him, even if she had heard something. Mrs. Barker was a force to be reckoned with, an observation that made him glance at the clock. He supposed Mrs. Barker was downstairs in the sitting room, fuming because he had detained Rosemary for so long. He therefore quickly broached the last subject on his mental list.

"Tell me, Rosemary, did Lord Ashe ever receive letters?"

"All the time, sir. I believe he was very liked by his friends. There were always invitations to dinners and concerts arriving at the door."

"And did he ever ask you to deliver a letter for him?"

"Oh, no, sir. That is not my job. He would have asked Mrs. Barker to find him a messenger."

"Yet sometimes, if one had a letter to deliver that one did not wish Mrs. Barker to know about, for some reason …"

When the girl did not rise to catch the bait, he asked, "Rosemary, I am going to ask you one more question, and the only reason why I must ask it is because it is so very important. Do you understand?"

"Yes, sir."

"When you were straightening up Lord Ashe's room, did you ever have occasion to read any letters that were left upon the table?"

For the first time the girl's face brightened into a smile. "You are a funny one, Mr. Bryght. Where would I have learned how to read?"

Theo Bryght laughed with the girl over his error, and then he sent her away. The moment she was gone, the smile disappeared from his face. This would be his last opportunity to look around the room. He could not stop Mrs. Barker from cleaning it and renting it out to someone new forever.

He looked under the sofa for a letter that might have gone astray, but there was nothing there. He performed the same chore under the bed. He then went to the wardrobe and searched through all the corners and drawers. Still there was nothing.

Next he contemplated his second quandary. He was not sure how the murderer — if there had been a murder — had entered and left the room. He supposed the person was known to Lord Ashe, and so the most likely scenario was that the two had entered the lodging house together. Perhaps the murderer, if he was also a blackmailer, had asked Lord Ashe to write a note that could be redeemed at a moneylender's place of business. After the note was in his hands, the murderer could have done the deed. Slashing a person's wrist was not the easiest way to kill a person, but it was quieter than a gun. If Lord Ashe had been ill, as the servant girl had suggested, he might have been too weak to resist the attempt on his life. And then …

Would the murderer have let himself out by the front door? Surely that was taking a risk. He could not know if Mrs. Barker or another servant would still be awake. Yet it was unlikely that he would leave by the window. Or was it?

Theo Bryght had examined the window before, but he gave it another look. A man could jump down from it to the street below, if he did not mind the possibility of breaking his legs or neck. No, the man must have left by the front door. But why did no one see him either enter or leave? Where were nosy servants when a person needed them?!

The Runner left the room and closed the door behind him. It was no use pretending otherwise, this case had defeated him. As he passed by the open door of the sitting room, he called out his thanks to the proprietress of the establishment and informed her she could now do with the room as she wished.

Once out upon the street, he considered what to do next. His leave was almost over. He could therefore return to London and restore the inquiry to Constable Brickwall's incompetent hands. Yet he hated to leave an inquiry unsolved.

"Mr. Bryght! Mr. Bryght!"

Theo Bryght turned to see who was calling his name. It was the yellow-toothed assistant. Apparently the assistant did not do much running while on the job, for the man was quite out of breath.

"Mr. Bryght," he repeated for a third time, once he reached the Runner, "I've been looking all over for you. Constable says you're to come at once. Something important has turned up."

IV.

Constable Brickwall was smoking his pipe by the fire when Theo Bryght entered the room, the very picture of contented indolence.

"Something has turned up?" asked the Runner.

"And without my running after it," replied the Constable, with a chuckle, enjoying his own wit.

"Would you like to share the joke?"

"He's over there." Constable Brickwall pointed toward the other side of the room, where a boy who looked to be about twelve or thirteen was fidgeting. "Tell this man what you know, laddie."

"You're the Runner from London?" asked the boy.

"Yes, I am. My name is Theo Bryght. With whom do I have the pleasure of speaking?"

"Tom is my name."

"And what would you like to tell me, Tom?"

"I was the one who found Lord Lauferby under the table, not Mr. Smythe."

"Ah, I see. What else would you like to tell me?"

"Lord Lauferby's hat and his purse were also there. But I didn't take anything."

"Nothing worth taking, I suppose, eh, laddie?" the Constable interjected.

"That's right," said Tom. "Not much blunt was there, considering it was a gentleman's purse. And the only other thing in it was a bit of paper with some writing on it. Vowels is what they call it."

Theo Bryght nodded his head. Lord Lauferby had mentioned that his vowels had been returned to his purse at some point during the night.

"But that's only partly why I've come here," the boy continued.

"You found something else under the table?" asked Theo Bryght.

"No, sir, not under the table. It was on the ground, beside the steps. I found it when I left in the morning. The morning after …"

The boy made a gesture of slashing his throat. Apparently he had been apprised of only a few facts concerning the case, but that lack of knowledge in no way obstructed his moment of triumph; for he could see the Bow Street Runner from London was listening to what he had to say with interest.

"Why have you said nothing before this?" asked the Runner.

"I would have showed it to you the first time you came around to the gaming hell, Mr. Bryght, only Mr. Smythe wouldn't let me talk to you."

"Well, you can tell me now. What exactly did you find, Tom?"

Tom pulled out of his pocket a small leather-bound diary, which he handed over to the Runner.

Theo Bryght opened it to the first page, where there were written the words: Property of Percy Ainsford Foster, Viscount Ashe. Next the Runner thumbed through the entries until he found the day of the murder. He saw an entry for a social call to be paid in the afternoon and the entry for the dinner engagement at Lord Lauferby's. After that there was another entry: an appointment at two o'clock in the morning.

The late hour was surprising. But even more surprising was the name of the person that Lord Ashe was supposed to have met.

"Thank you, Tom. You did the right thing by coming here," he said and slipped a coin into the boy's hand.

"Find something interesting in that book?" asked Constable Brickwall, after Tom left.

"Yes, I believe I did," Theo Bryght replied. He slipped the diary into his coat pocket and went quickly toward the door.

"Where are you rushing to now?" asked the constable, who had watched the London man's running about Brighton with distinct disapproval.

"Yorkshire!"

CANTO THE FOURTH

If Theo Bryght did not approve of Lord Lauferby's dandyism, he did approve of the young man's loyalty to his friends, both those who were dead and those, like himself, who were still among the living. As soon as the Runner had expressed a wish to travel to Yorkshire and continue his inquiries there, Lord Lauferby had offered the services of his carriage and team of four horses, which would take them through the first stage of their journey at a fast clip. From there on they would need fresh horses, but Lord Lauferby generously agreed to pay the bill for that, as well as all their other traveling expenses.

"Had some luck at the gaming hell," he explained. "A person cannot lose every night, you know."

During their journey Theo Bryght was reminded of how comfortable such travel could be, when one had the money to travel in style. But despite the debt of gratitude he owed to the young lord, he did not reveal the entire reason for his hasty decision to leave Brighton, which was the entry in Lord Ashe's diary. He did not quite trust the young man's ability to keep a secret, especially when he was tipsy, an occurrence that repeated itself practically every night.

Bryght was also not entirely convinced Lauferby was really the "tulip" he professed to be. It was not unheard of for a cunning criminal to pretend to be a harmless imbecile. Lauferby's unashamed talk about his gambling and his drinking might be due to a nature that was truly open and unguarded. Or it could all be a show, a performance to take the suspicion away from him and put it on someone else. The revelation of the note, with its one-word message, might also have been a trick to send the Runner running after the wrong scent. Theo Bryght had therefore said only that he had finished his inquiries in the resort town and would be continuing them in the Yorkshire moors.

There was another reason, though, why he was reluctant to talk about the diary and the new light it possibly threw upon the inquiry. He was not quite sure, himself, what to think.

Despite the words spoken in his interview with Lady Ashe, the Runner had never seriously considered that Lord March had committed the murder. Theo Bryght did not personally know the March family, but he had thought he had heard enough to form a reasonable opinion about the man. The Dowager and her son mainly stayed on their Yorkshire estate and made only brief, obligatory visits to London and Brighton during those two fair cities' respective seasons.

It had not always been so. Shortly after the present Lord March inherited his titles and estates, he had been a frequent visitor to the most brilliant homes and assembly rooms, where he was the subject of more than the usual gossip and speculation, due to his vast wealth and his still unmarried state.

But as the years dragged on and no lady appeared on the social scene who could meet with his approval, society gradually lost interest in his comings and goings.

He was still invited, of course, to all the best dinners and balls, just as he had membership in all of the most exclusive gentlemen's clubs. But whereas Lord Ashe was considered to be a "splendid fellow" in that glittering social circle known as the *ton*, Lord March was thought to be the opposite: too high in the instep, too big of a bore. His absence from society, which occurred more frequently with each passing year, was therefore rarely remarked upon.

However, the entry in the diary was not some figment of Theo Bryght's imagination. It was written in black ink upon a white page. If Lord March's interest in the affair was solely to make the suicide look like a murder — the Runner's original assumption — how was one to account for the early morning appointment? He somehow had to fit this new piece of information into his still unfinished puzzle.

Although it was not unusual for the Beau Monde to drink, dance, and gamble away the entire night — dropping into their beds only when the sun began its daily ascent — it was less common to do serious business at such a late hour. Therefore, although the two o'clock appointment might have been of an entirely innocent and innocuous nature — perhaps to discuss the purchase of a horse or the need to mend a fence bordering the perimeter of their two estates — it was highly unlikely. Yet it could not have been meant to be a secret meeting, since Lord Ashe wrote it down in his diary.

It made no sense, unless the entry was … what? Did Lord Ashe suspect the appointment might turn deadly? Was the entry meant to be a finger from the grave that would point to his murderer, should his fears prove to be justified? That was a chilling thought, especially since Theo Bryght could feel the diary, which was safely stowed in his coat pocket, pressing against his heart.

"I still wish I knew what it meant. Have you no idea at all, Bryght?"

Theo Bryght roused himself from his own thoughts and turned to his companion.

"It must mean something, Spain," Lord Lauferby continued. "People do not send letters with just one word, unless it is a prank of some sort."

There it was again, the one-word letter. Was Lord Lauferby truly as concerned as he looked? Or was he trying to ferret out information, to find out the Runner's thoughts? And what would the "tulip" think if he were aware that at this moment the Runner was considering the reasons why a young man like Lord Lauferby might murder his friend? It was very convenient for Lauferby that his vowels had been returned to his purse, but was it true they were returned to him without his notice, while he was under the influence of too much drink? Was it not possible that he was the sort of man who would steal his vowels from his creditor's purse and then kill the man who threatened to expose him? Some people would do anything when they were desperate for money or their honor was at stake. However, the Runner's instincts told him it was highly unlikely Lauferby would do anything that might risk spoiling the flawless beauty of his intricate cravat, and so he replied, "Perhaps that explains it. Are any of the men from your former regiment the type to play a prank?"

"It is hard to know. There is one thing, though, I am certain of. If this is a prank, the letter did not come from Lord March."

"He was an officer in your regiment?"

"Yes."

"Lord March and Lord Ashe were related, were they not?"

"Second cousins, I believe, or third. I do not remember. But they did not get along."

"In Spain?"

"Yes, in Spain. In England Ashe was better able to keep his distance from the March family."

"I was under the impression their estates were adjacent."

"They are, but Ashe spent most of his time in London or Brighton or visiting the estates of his friends."

"What happened in Spain? Did they quarrel?"

"It was ridiculous, really, when I think back upon it, now I am older. Older and wiser, you know."

When Bryght said nothing, Lord Lauferby continued with his story. "We were on the road, traveling to meet another regiment, when we rode right into a trap, a regular ambush. Several of our men were killed on the spot. A few of us were badly wounded."

"Who was that?"

"Besides me there was Ashe and Lord March and the batman."

"John Collins?"

"Yes. There were one or two other regular soldiers, but I do not remember their names."

"What happened after that?"

"The wounded were taken to a nearby village. I do not remember being transported there; I must have fainted from my wounds. But when I woke up, we were all settled comfortably in a barn that had been turned into a kind of hospital."

"The villagers took good care of you?"

"It was really just one family, I believe. And this family had a very pretty daughter. She would bring us water and help us eat our food. Her mother was always there, too, of course."

"And so you fell in love with this pretty young lady?"

"Not me. Lord March."

Theo Bryght stared at his companion, not sure if he should believe the young man or not. Unless he had misread Lord March entirely, it seemed highly unlikely a snob of his caliber would stoop so low as to fall in love with a simple village girl.

"If it had happened in England, I would quite agree," said Lord Lauferby, after Theo Bryght had voiced his objection. "But it is different when you are in a strange country, and feverish to boot. When the girl offered you a cup of water, it tasted like it had come straight from a river in Eden."

"Very well, let us suppose Lord March did fall in love with a village girl. What did that have to do with Lord Ashe?"

"When we began to feel better Ashe thought he might have some fun, to pass the time. And so he made the girl fall in love with him."

"He could do that easily, I suppose?"

"Ashe had a way with the young ladies. And Lord March must have been over thirty, even back then. Practically an old man."

Theo Bryght decided to let those last words pass without comment. "That was the cause of their quarrel, this girl?" he asked, still not believing the story.

"Not the girl. But you met Lord March. Surely you saw he is not the type who would enjoy being made a fool of."

That made more sense, Theo Bryght had to admit. Lord March would not appreciate being bested in a flirtation, even if the flirtation meant very little to him. But was he the type of man to bear a grudge? And would he commit murder for such a trivial reason? Theo Bryght thought not. Wishing to secure ownership of Ramblewood, before Ashe gambled the family estate away, was a much more likely motive, if one were to cast Lord March in the role of criminal.

Regardless of the motive, though, it was hard to imagine Lord March doing the deed himself. It was much more likely that he would engage the services of some old and trusted servant, someone who was so bound by ties of loyalty and affection to the family that he would think nothing of removing an obstacle to the family's continued good name and fortune, if requested by his master to do so. Then, after the first murder had been committed, March might find a way to quietly remove the servant from the earthly ties that prevented the man's soul from ascending to heaven.

That theory, though, did not account for the early-morning appointment written down in Ashe's diary. There had to be a reason why the estranged cousins had arranged a meeting at such an unusual hour. And since it now appeared Lord March was the last person to see Lord Ashe alive, Theo Bryght was determined to find out what that reason was.

II.

Charlotte and Mrs. Seymour were still at their breakfast when a boy from the village came running up to their door.

"A letter for you, Lady Ashe," he called out, his face flushed from both his run and his excitement. "Coachman says you must reply at once, if you want it to go in the mail today."

Charlotte hurriedly opened the letter. To her relief it was not more bad news.

"What is it, Charlotte?" asked Mrs. Seymour, who had also come to the door.

"An invitation." Charlotte slipped a small coin into the boy's hand and said, "Please tell the coachman thank you, but there is no need for him to wait. I will send a reply with tomorrow's mail coach."

The boy hurried back to the village, and Charlotte and Mrs. Seymour returned to their meal.

"An invitation from whom?" asked Mrs. Seymour.

"Lady March."

"Lady March?"

"She has invited us to Lundsmoor Park."

Mrs. Seymour sat with her piece of toast suspended in mid-air, unsure as to what her reaction should be. Normally an invitation to a great house such as Lundsmoor Park would be an occasion for great joy. But this was not the season for house parties. And the unpleasant incident of the four thousand pounds further aroused her suspicions.

"Do you intend to go, Charlotte?"

"I do not know."

After breakfast Charlotte decided to take a long walk on the moors. Her thoughts were always clearer when she was surrounded by nothing but the fields and the open skies.

It was the first time, she realized, she had walked further than the village since moving to the cottage. Before, when she had walked on the moors, she had walked them as an owner. The land and the sheep and cows had all belonged to her grandfather. After he died, they had belonged to her. She had had a place in the world, and a place in society, which had come from owning the land. Now the livestock still belonged to the land — they had a right and a reason to be there — but she did not. She was only a visitor. Her right to traverse the hills was the same right that belonged to anyone in the village or any anonymous traveler who passed down the road, on the way from somewhere to someplace else.

'Thus let me live, unheard, unknown; Thus unlamented let me die; Steal from the world, and not a stone tell where I lie,' she whispered, quoting the final stanza from the poem by Pope. When she had first come across the poem, while still a girl living at Hopewell, she had found its air of lonely melancholy to be romantic. But now that she was an anonymous traveler, herself, on the moors, banished from that childhood world and everything in that was dear, the words suddenly sounded falsely sentimental. Privacy she would always treasure. But she did not wish to live unheard, she wanted to shout. She did not wish to die alone and unlamented, she wanted to cry. But what could she do? She would not even be able to live in the cottage if it were not for her aunt's two hundred pounds a year.

Her thoughts returned to the invitation from Lady March. Like her aunt, she too regarded the invitation with suspicion. She did not believe the invitation signaled some new danger, but it was very possible that to accept the invitation would only invite further humiliation. Perhaps Lady March intended to offer her the position of paid companion. Or, even worse, perhaps the elderly woman had found her a position in some stately home as governess.

Charlotte grimaced at the thought. Yet if that were the case, there was no reason to invite Charlotte and Mrs. Seymour to Lundsmoor Park. The subject could have been broached in a letter just as easily and with less pain.

Perhaps, then, Lady March was lonely and wanted company. It would not do to have a large party so soon after a death in the family. So perhaps that was why the invitation had been extended to her and Mrs. Seymour.

They were family, in a matter of speaking, and so society could not disapprove. Yet the three ladies did not yet know one other well enough to be bored by the other's company.

Or perhaps there was another reason entirely. She would not know, unless she agreed to go — and her instincts told her not to shut a door before she knew what was on the other side. Perhaps there was a way Charlotte could turn the visit to her advantage. How, she did not know, because she could not see a way out of her predicament.

Yet if she did accept the invitation, she would be expected to stay at Lundsmoor Park for at least a few weeks. And if she left Butterhill, she would not see …

She stopped and looked around her. She had not realized she had walked so far. Were she to continue along the path she had taken she would reach Hopewell — and that she must not do. John Collins had not called on them again, after the outing to Whitby. She was not entirely surprised, when she recalled her behaviour. And she could only commend his behaviour, for there was clearly no reason for them to continue the acquaintanceship. He was a married man, even though it was an unhappy marriage. She was a respectable widow.

No, there was no reason to expect him to call again. And so there was no reason for her to decline the invitation to Lundsmoor Park on his account. Indeed, it might be better to go and occupy her mind with the gardens of a new vista. She would take her sketching pad, and pretend she was interested in the view, as though a view mattered when one had no one to share it with.

She stood for a few more moments gazing in the direction of Hopewell. She must learn to think of it as just another great house, she knew, one of the dozens that dotted the moors.

A carriage driving down the road disturbed this attempt at noble self-denial. She turned in time to see a woman's hand emerge from the carriage window, and to see a glove drop from that hand onto the ground. The carriage continued on its way, without stopping, and quickly disappeared from view.

Charlotte went to the road to retrieve the glove. When she picked it up, she noticed something had been secreted inside it — a note that had been folded into a small square. She unfolded the page and read:

Here. Tomorrow. At this hour.

Although there was no signature, Charlotte believed she knew who the author of the note was. The carriage belonged to Hopewell. There was only one person belonging to that house who would have a lady's glove. The author, therefore, must be Mrs. Collins. But why should she wish to meet with Charlotte, and arrange the meeting in such an odd way?

Charlotte recalled the words of Mr. Collins, that the mind of his wife had become sadly deranged. Yet even such a one must at times feel lonely. Most likely, Mrs. Collins, having seen some unknown female walking upon the moors, had become possessed of an urge to engage in female company and the deterioration of her mind had made it seem proper to arrange a meeting in such a manner. Moved by both pity and curiosity, Charlotte resolved to do as the unfortunate woman wished, and return to the same spot the next day.

III.

The next morning Charlotte sent off two letters. The first was to the Bow Street Runner, informing him of the arrival of John Collins in the neighborhood and of her own imminent removal to Lundsmoor Park. The second was to Lady March, accepting her invitation.

Although Charlotte did not need to worry about her wardrobe — mourning clothes could be without decoration — Mrs. Seymour was sent all in a flutter about the state of her own attire. And so while her aunt and Ella were discussing new trim for a bonnet, Charlotte was able to slip out of the house for another long walk practically unnoticed. The glove, which she intended to return to Mrs. Collins when they met, was safely tucked away in the sleeve of her pelisse.

When she reached the appointed place she found a ledge to sit upon that was placed not too far from the road. It would seem natural, should anyone pass by, to find her resting there. No one would suspect the storm that was brewing in her mind, or that her earlier feelings of pity had been replaced by emotions that were much less admirable.

"It is unfair!" she wanted to scream. "Why must we all suffer and suffer for the rest of our lives — or at least until Mrs. Collins is no longer alive?"

No longer alive. Was there a glimmer of hope in those words, she wondered. Could it be that Mrs. Collins suffered a weakness of the body, as well as the mind, that would prevent the woman from living out the normal span of a person's days? While Charlotte knew she should react in horror to contemplating such thoughts for even an instant, she could not stop herself from thinking them. All she wanted was a husband to love and admire and serve, and the more her thoughts returned to that day in Whitby — and they returned there at least several times every day — the more she was convinced her one chance for happiness lay with John Collins. They shared a similar social background, a similar desire to do what was right and good. Could it really be her fate to be continually aware that her happiness was so close, and yet impossible to grasp?

The sound of carriage wheels made her stand up with a start. In a moment she would see, face to face, the woman who was her unwitting rival. Unwitting. Charlotte was suddenly overpowered by a feeling of shame. How must this woman feel, trapped as she was inside a horror not of her own making? How many times had *she* wished to scream, knowing in her lucid hours that her husband's love was fled, chased away by a mad demon crueler than death?

The carriage rolled to a stop. A woman's gloved hand motioned to Charlotte to approach the carriage, and Charlotte obeyed the summons. When she looked through the open window, Charlotte felt her heart break, both for herself and the woman who sat opposite her. Mrs. Collins, although no longer in the first bloom of youth, was a beauty — an exotic beauty with striking jet-black hair, flashing dark eyes, and a flawless complexion. Charlotte could understand why John Collins had fallen in love with the woman — and in her heart she believed that at least a small part of the man must love her still.

"Lady Ashe?"

Charlotte noted the woman spoke with a slight lilt.

Before more could be said, the elderly woman companion dozing in the corner of the carriage woke up. After pushing Mrs. Collins away from the window, the grey-haired fury shouted to the coachman in a language Charlotte did not understand. The horses sprang into motion. A moment later they were gone.

IV.

"It is really too distressing. Charlotte?"

"Yes, Auntie?" Charlotte forced herself to reply. Although the physical distance separating her from Mrs. Seymour was no more than the width of their small dining table, where a light supper was being served, Charlotte's thoughts had been very far away.

"I do hope you have not caught a chill," said Mrs. Seymour. "You have not been yourself since you returned from your walk. I would retire early tonight, my dear."

"Perhaps I shall. But you were saying, Auntie, that something is distressing?"

"I cannot find my tooth powder anywhere, and there is so much to do before we go to Lundsmoor Park that I really cannot ask Ella to go to the village tomorrow."

"I shall go for you, Auntie."

"But if you are not feeling well?"

"I shall be fine after a good night's sleep."

Sleep, however, eluded her. She was both disappointed and disturbed by her appointment with Mrs. Collins. Disappointed because the woman — who had seemed, to Charlotte's inexpert eye, perfectly lucid — clearly had wanted to speak with her and Charlotte would have given much to have learned what she had meant to say; disturbed because Mrs. Collins certainly had not deserved the rough treatment given her by the companion. Charlotte had not been in any danger, and so she was sorry if her mere presence by the carriage had resulted in harm to the unfortunate woman.

She felt Mr. Collins must be informed, yet how could she broach the subject in a tactful way, especially when there was no contact between the two houses? No one appreciated interference, no matter how kindly meant. And Mr. Collins had made it perfectly clear during their first meeting that he did not wish Charlotte and his wife to become acquainted.

However, it might be that Mr. Collins was not aware the woman he had hired to be a companion to his wife was unsuitable for her task. Men often were not aware of what went on in the servants' quarters, or behind closed doors. And he was new to being the master of a large household, which put him at an additional disadvantage.

Charlotte therefore felt she must speak. But what excuse could she give for visiting Hopewell?

The morning did not bring with it an answer to her dilemma. She therefore reluctantly accepted the only solution that had come to her — the return of a book to the Hopewell library — and set off for the village after breakfast.

The purchase of the tooth powder was easily accomplished. She continued along the village street. Not long after she had left the village behind and was on the road that led to the Hopewell moors she heard the wheels of an approaching carriage. The sound made her quickly turn around. Perhaps she would have a second change to engage Mrs. Collins in conversation, and this time they would be more successful.

However, it was only the dogcart of Mr. Stephens, the area's only surgeon. He brought his horse to a stop and said, "Good morning, Lady Ashe. May I offer you a ride?"

Charlotte hesitated. She did not wish the surgeon to know she was walking to Hopewell, and so the safest course was to decline his offer. Yet there was a reason to accept it: the surgeon might know something about the malady afflicting Mrs. Collins. Charlotte therefore accepted the surgeon's offer, saying, "Are you going as far as the Hopewell moors, Mr. Stephens?"

"And further," he replied. "Old Mrs. Crowley was taken ill during the night."

"I am sorry to hear that."

They rode for a little while in silence. To her consternation, Charlotte could think of no way to bring up the subject of Mrs. Collins without appearing to be an insufferable gossip. To her relief, the doctor broached the topic first.

"If you are going to Hopewell to pay a visit to Mrs. Collins," he said, "I am afraid you will be disappointed."

"Why is that?"

"From what I hear, she does not receive visitors. She is ill."

"Yes, I have heard. My aunt and I are quite worried. We are hoping there is something we can do to relieve the lady's distress. Have you seen Mrs. Collins?"

"No. It is an illness of the mind, according to Mr. Collins. Since my art does not extend so far, Mr. Collins saw no reason for me to see the lady."

They rode in silence for a little longer, and then the doctor added, "I can leave you here, Lady Ashe, if you have changed your mind about visiting Hopewell."

"Why should I do that, Mr. Stephens?"

"There was some talk in the village. Some people saw you and Mr. Collins traveling together in the same carriage."

"Mrs. Seymour was also in the carriage, Mr. Stephens. Mr. Collins was kind enough to offer the use of his carriage so my aunt and I could travel to Whitby."

"That may very well be. But the people were not gossiping about your aunt."

"And if people see me riding in your dogcart, will they gossip about us?"

"I am a married man and old enough to be your father. Mr. Collins is a young man, and a good-looking one at that. I am only offering you advice, Lady Ashe, as a long-time acquaintance of your family. There is nothing for you at Hopewell, not anymore."

"I am of the same opinion. But I discovered a book in my trunk that belongs to the library. Surely there is no harm in my wishing to return something that is not mine to keep?"

Even to her own ears, her words sounded false. She was therefore grateful the surgeon chose to say nothing more on the subject.

When they reached the point in the road where the long avenue to Hopewell began, Charlotte descended. "Please send my wishes for a speedy recovery to Mrs. Crowley," she said to the surgeon, hoping to convey an air of cheerful confidence that she did not truly feel.

Instead of driving off at once the surgeon waited, apparently hopeful she might still change her mind. Charlotte, however, continued up the familiar path.

When the house came into view, she stopped and took a deep breath. Nothing had been changed, and for that she was grateful. The house still retained its air of gentle grandeur — more like an elderly duchess who has the confidence to gracefully acknowledge that her day has passed than a young beauty who is all dazzling paint and hard polish.

Working in the front lawn was the head gardener, Luke, who was turning the soil in one of the flower beds. She greeted him as though it were the most natural thing in the world that she should be there. She was not sure what was truly going through his mind, but he took his cue and went to the front door to announce her presence to the servants, so she would not have to suffer the embarrassment of seeing their surprise.

Soon afterward the butler, who had come to Hopewell when she was a small child, hurried out to greet her and show her into the front drawing room. "I shall tell Mr. Collins that you are here, my lady."

"Mr. Collins is in, then?"

"Yes, my lady."

The butler left, and Charlotte was grateful to have a few minutes to compose her thoughts. She could not deny that she wished to see Mr. Collins again. Yet she knew her coming to Hopewell without an invitation — no matter how just or laudable the reason for her visit — must lower her in his eyes.

Footsteps approached the door. She turned. Mr. Collins entered the room.

She could not help but notice how natural he appeared, how very much he looked the part of the owner of the house. If one did not know the truth, one would never have suspected he had not been born to the role fortune had favored him to play. And she thought how odd the world was, really. Although breeding did matter, there were many instances where all the town polish in the world could not hide the coarseness of a highly-born but debased soul, just as there were people born into the lower classes who possessed a spirit that was noble and refined. No, the days when she might have hated him for usurping her place were dead and buried. Hopewell suited him, as well as it had suited her. The only pity was that Hopewell could not suit them together.

"My apologies, Lady Ashe, for keeping you waiting. I did not hear your carriage."

"I walked part of the way. It is a very pleasant day for a walk."

"You must be thirsty then. May I offer you some refreshments?"

"I only came to give you this, Mr. Collins." She handed him the book she had brought with her. "I found it among my other books. It belongs to the Hopewell library, and so I wanted to return it."

"There was no need. It will take me many years to read all the books that are there already."

"Yes, but I believe it is part of a set. It would be a shame if someone were to go looking for this volume and not find it."

He took the book and placed it on a nearby table. He did not speak. She knew she should now state the true reason for her visit. Instead, she said, "Mrs. Seymour and I will be going to Lundsmoor Park for a few weeks."

"That is the home of Lord March, is it not?"

"Lady March invited us for a visit."

"I hope you and Mrs. Seymour will enjoy your stay.

"The house is considered to be quite exceptional, and there are many interesting views."

Before she could continue with more inanities, Mr. Collins stopped her and said, "Why have you come here, Lady Ashe? I am quite sure it was not to return a book no one missed and very few will ever read."

When she did not speak, he said, "Perhaps it was to return a glove?"

"A glove?" she asked, hoping she had not betrayed her surprise.

"Yes, my wife lost one of her gloves a few days ago, when she was taking a drive on the moors."

Finally finding her courage, Charlotte said, "Mr. Collins ..."

But before she could say more, he stopped her and said, "I know you must think me cruel for not allowing my wife to enjoy the pleasure of your company, and that of your aunt. But you must believe me when I say it is impossible. You see, sometimes my wife can appear to be almost lucid. But when the mood is upon her, and the change can happen in an instant, she becomes violent.

That is why her companion must be with her at all times. To some eyes, Maria might seem almost cruel in her treatment of my wife. But those who understand my wife's illness know Maria is an invaluable servant. More than once my wife has attempted to take her own life, and mine. Maria prevents my wife from accomplishing her purpose."

Until this point he had been looking at a wall, a picture, a sofa — at any point in the room except at Charlotte. Now, however, he permitted his eyes to rest upon her face.

"I would never forgive myself, Lady Ashe, if I allowed Mrs. Collins to see you, and she fell into one of her rages and did you harm."

"I did not realize ... I am sorry to have disturbed you, Mr. Collins. Please forgive my intrusion."

Charlotte moved toward the door, but before she could reach it he again stopped her. Speaking this time in a lowered voice, he said, "There is no reason to apologize, Lady Ashe. I only wish it were possible for there be to be more intrusions such as this. But it is not possible. Your reputation is dearer to me than my own life. I must therefore ask you not to come here again, for your sake."

They walked down the hallway, in silence. Mr. Collins also accompanied her part of the way down the path that led to the country road. When they reached a place where they could not be overheard, he removed a letter from his coat pocket. "I found this sitting on the desk in the library the other day. None of the servants seem to know how it got here."

He showed her the page. There was just one word written on it: Spain.

"Have you seen it before? I thought it might have fallen out of a book, when the parlour maid was in the room dusting."

"No, I do not recall ever seeing such a letter," Charlotte replied.

"I suppose it is nothing, but it did strike me as odd the way it seemed to turn up out of nowhere. I hope it is not a prank."

"A prank?"

"People can be cruel, especially in a country village, where there is always so much gossip."

"You think, then, that it refers to your time in Spain?

"Someone was bound to find out I was once Lord Ashe's valet."

"But what can that matter to anyone in Butterhill?"

"It would matter to someone who believed I have no right to be the owner of Hopewell, or to admire Hopewell's former mistress. Good-bye, Lady Ashe."

V.

Lady March, having come to the end of the shrubbery, turned and began to walk down the length of the path again. Although the sun had disappeared behind a cloud and the summer breeze had turned chilly, she had no desire to go inside. There would be time enough after supper to yawn by the fire.

In the distance she could see her son, Lord March, returning to the stables. She was proud that her son took his duties as landholder so seriously. The tenants on their property certainly had nothing to complain of. At the first sign of a leak in a roof or a clogged drain, Lord March saddled his horse and went to inspect the damage himself. Repairs were made, and improvements, as well, as if it were he — and not the tenant's family — who was living in the structure.

Her only complaint was that her son had never married. One day he would, she was sure. With privilege came duties, and he had a duty to produce an heir. But if he did not marry soon, she might not have the opportunity to see the successor to the title.

Age had not dulled her wonderment at the fact that her only son had not married. It was her first thought in the morning, her last at night. She had forgiven him, in his youth, for being too proud, too conscious of his own worth and too unwilling to forgive the imperfections of others. But people, as they matured, usually learned to accept the world for what it was — a place of fleeting pleasures and imperfect joys. A woman did not have to be perfect to be an acceptable wife. She needed only reasonably good looks and the good sense not to be a chatterbox. And a title, of course. The March family could provide the fortune, but good breeding was essential.

That, of course, was the problem with Lady Ashe. The fact that her fortune had been lost could be forgiven, especially since it had been a relative of the March family who had lost it. But she was a tradesman's granddaughter. Her title was bought, not borne in her blood. Yet she might do. And this was a better solution to the heir problem than the solution offered by Lady Cunningham, which was to marry off her daughter Odelia to Lord March.

Odelia Cunningham was in many ways a good catch — pretty without being so pretty that she was frivolous and vain; talented at the pianoforte but with enough social finesse to know when it was time to stop playing and move to the card table; intelligent without being bookish and overly enthusiastic about that Lord Byron who was making such a nuisance of himself in society.

The Cunningham title was not a particularly old one, but it had not been newly minted either. And if the family fortune was not large, it did include some rather good property.

The one obstacle was the young lady's age, and she was very young. Sixteen was much too young for a man like Lord March, who needed a wife who could also be a companion and not just another pretty pet. And so that brought Lady March's thoughts back to Lady Ashe.

"You look pensive, Ma'am. I trust you have not heard bad news."

Lord March had entered the shrubbery. Lady March was pleased to see he was still a fine-looking man. There was only a hint of the decay that came to all men as they approached their fortieth year.

"On the contrary. Lady Ashe has accepted my invitation. I think the room overlooking the rose garden will suit her very nicely."

Lord March merely bowed. Domestic matters such as these held little interest for him.

"March, I have been thinking about that Bow Street Runner. Have you heard from him?"

"No. I assume he will write only if he has news."

"And do you think he will ever have news?"

"I think that if he has not yet discovered the true cause of Ashe's death, he may never do so."

Lord March gave his arm to his mother, and the two walked toward the house. As they often did, they walked together in a comfortable silence. When they came upon a view that afforded a distant glimpse of the outer rim of trees that marked the end of their estate and the beginning of the property belonging to the Ashe family at Ramblewood, they stopped. There was no need to speak.

VI.

The carriage bearing Theo Bryght and Lord Lauferby rumbled down Butterhill's one street and pulled to a halt in front of the apothecary's shop. Bryght alighted from the carriage, while his traveling companion remained inside, asleep.

"Is there a letter for me?" he asked the owner of the shop. Before leaving Brighton he had written to a colleague in London with connections on the Stock Exchange, asking for information about how Mr. Collins had made his fortune. He was pleased to see that the reply was waiting for him. After paying for the letter, he asked the proprietor for directions to the cottage where Lady Ashe was staying.

"I can give them to you, but you will not find her there," replied Mr. Hearn. "Nor will you find Mrs. Seymour, for that matter."

"But I suppose you know where they have gone to," replied the Runner. "I have come on a matter of some importance."

The apothecary glanced out the window and saw the elegant carriage and team of four horses standing in the street. He also noticed the fine livery of the two coachmen who sat on the front bench and the tiger — the young groom who was dressed in the traditional yellow and black striped waistcoat of his profession — who sat at the back. He therefore said, without further ado, "They have all gone to Lundsmoor Park."

Theo Bryght thanked the man for the information and returned to the carriage. He was unsure what to do next. He now had another item to add to his long list of things that made him unhappy with this inquiry: Lady Ashe was at Lundsmoor Park. He did not think she was in danger. But since he was still in the dark about so many things, he could not assure himself that she was perfectly safe, either.

His first thought, therefore, was to continue to the March family's ancestral home as quickly as possible. Yet in addition to advising Lady Ashe about the state of the inquiry into her husband's death, he had intended to call upon John Collins — for he had learned that Collins had moved to Hopewell without the assistance of Lady Ashe's letter, which was waiting for him in Brighton, unbeknownst to him. But before he paid a visit to Hopewell, Bryght wanted to read his letter and so, after ensuring that Lord Lauferby was still fast asleep, he opened it and quickly read through the letter's contents.

Those contents confirmed what he already knew: Mr. Collins, through remarkable good luck, had made his fortune on the Stock Exchange. The letter also confirmed that it was generally known the former valet had more than once paid the vowels of Lord Ashe. The message ended with the information that it was not known who had purchased the sugar plantation in Jamaica and under what circumstances it was sold. It was also not known under what terms Mr. Collins had become the owner of Hopewell, although the talk in the gentlemen's clubs, which was repeated in the coffee houses, was that it had been given to Mr. Collins as a gift, in lieu of a payment in cash, for gambling debts incurred by Lord Ashe.

Theo Bryght put the letter in his pocket just a moment before Lord Lauferby awoke from his sleep and lazily looked around.

"Why have we stopped?"

"We are in Butterhill."

"I hope Butterhill has a reasonably good inn. My bones have taken a basting."

"I have discovered that Lady Ashe is at Lundsmoor Park."

"Lord March's estate? Let us go there, Bryght. We shall be much more comfortable at Lundsmoor Park than here."

"I agree, but first I would like to see John Collins."

"Oh. That is a bit awkward for me, socially, you know."

"You may wait in the carriage."

"No, I have come to see the whole show. I know. I shall make an excuse that I wish to repay him the money I owe. That will make things right."

Theo Bryght gave an inward sigh. He was glad to be out of the false world of the *ton*, where one could borrow money from anyone but pay a social call to only a select few. True, he sometimes missed certain comforts and privileges – such as a private carriage and hot water at his beck and call, and he was yearning for a hot bath after their long day's travel – but he would not trade them for the anonymity he currently enjoyed. When dressed in his Runner's clothes and swagger, no one paid him the least bit of attention. He was invisible. He could come and go as he pleased, talk with whom he wanted and ignore those whom he wished to ignore, without worrying that his standing in society would be lowered since he was already at the bottom. It was a freedom few people achieved in life. Of course, in a world where most people were clawing their way up the social ladder, it was a freedom that was seldom strived for.

Those thoughts carried him to Hopewell. When they arrived, they were informed that Mr. Collins was not in. "But he is expected back shortly," said the butler. "Would you like to wait for him in the drawing room?"

As the butler had accompanied his words with a gesture that led to a doorway in the front part of the house, Theo Bryght replied, "We would prefer to wait in the library."

The butler complied by showing them to the back of the house. When the door had been closed behind them, Lord Lauferby, who had begun to become caught up in the spirit of the inquiry, asked, "What difference did the room make?"

"It is not the room, Lauferby, it is the door."

"What door?"

"This door," said the Runner, going to the door that led to the garden. "It is a trifle stuffy in here, is it not?" He then opened the door and walked outside.

"I did not notice a lack of air," Lord Lauferby replied, joining him on the terrace.

"Yet if Mr. Collins asks why we are outside, that is what we must tell him."

"I see. But why do we want to be outside and not inside, in the library?"

"Because Mrs. Collins is perhaps in the garden."

"I thought it was John Collins you wanted to see."

"It is. But are you not curious to see the new mistress of Hopewell? Or perhaps you already made her acquaintance in Brighton."

"I had not heard there was a Mrs. Collins until you mentioned her just now."

Theo Bryght stopped. Lord Lauferby had made a very good point. He had only assumed there was a Mrs. Collins, hoping that if the lady was of a talkative nature he might discover some valuable information before the master of the house came home.

The Runner surveyed the back of the house from his vantage point on the terrace. He could not imagine living in such a place alone. A house of this size would require a woman's touch, he felt, in order to give it life. It was possible, though, that John Collins was not married, in which case the matrons in the area with unmarried daughters must be all a-flutter.

He looked up to the upper floors. As he did so, he thought he saw a curtain close.

VII.

When John Collins returned to Hopewell the butler informed him that he had two visitors, who were waiting for his return in the library.

"Who are they?" he asked, depositing his gloves on the silver tray the butler had extended in his direction.

"Lord Lauferby, sir, and a Mister Theo Bryght."

"I shall want my meal served as soon as they are gone."

"They will not be staying for dinner?"

"No."

Having settled that point, the butler retreated to the servants' stairway and John Collins went into the library. He saw that the door to the terrace was open, and that the two men were standing outside, looking upward. Mr. Collins thought he knew what had attracted their attention, and he was not pleased by their intrusion into his private affairs. He therefore remained in the library and, without bothering to introduce himself, said, "There are no public viewing days at Hopewell, gentlemen, and so if you have any business with me please come inside and say what it is."

Mr. Bryght entered the room, followed by Lord Lauferby, who carefully closed the door behind them.

"A pity, because it is a charming house," said Theo Bryght. "And the grounds are lovely as well. The children must enjoy all the open space."

"I have no children. But I have had a long and tiring day. So I ask that you will do me the courtesy of stating your business at once." He then glanced over at Lord Lauferby and said, "If that business concerns a loan, I regret to inform you I am not able to accommodate your needs at the present time."

"Not all, Collins," said Lord Lauferby. "Quite the opposite, in fact. I thought I might owe you a small amount of blunt, and so I have come to pay you back."

"You owe me nothing, Lord Lauferby."

"But it was you who returned my vowels to me, was it not?"

"After you won the money at the gaming table and paid me back. I do know the rules, my lord."

"I won, did I?" he said, casting a glance over at the Runner. "I should have thought I would have remembered."

"I believe you returned to the table afterward and lost the rest of your winnings in the next play."

"That would explain it then, if it was fleeting as all that."

Theo Bryght had been following the conversation with interest and he now said to John Collins, "Then you also went to the gaming club, after Lord Lauferby's dinner party?"

"Yes, I was there," replied Mr. Collins. "I often accompanied Lord Ashe in the evenings."

"I assume you heard Lord Ashe was murdered later that night."

"I heard a rumor, the next morning, that he had commit suicide. But I was forced to leave Brighton on an early coach. I therefore missed most of the *on dit* that came afterward."

"If it was your impression Lord Ashe had commit suicide, why were you not surprised when I referred to it as murder?"

"I will be quite frank with you, Mr. Bryght. Lady Ashe has already informed me there is a theory that Lord Ashe was murdered. I assumed it was only a lady's fantasy. I was not aware you took her suspicions seriously."

"And I was not aware you are acquainted with Lady Ashe."

"We are neighbours, and Butterhill is a small village."

"Did Lady Ashe tell you who she suspected of doing the deed?"

"Lady Ashe is quite capable of speaking for herself."

"Very true, Mr. Collins. And who would you suspect?"

"I would suspect Lord Ashe, because I still believe it was suicide."

"Lord Ashe had no enemies?"

"None that I know of."

"And yet he is dead. Whether it was by suicide or by murder, Lord Ashe did not die a natural death. You cannot deny that."

"Nor should I wish to."

"He owed a great deal of money to many people, I understand."

"As do many gentlemen."

"Perhaps one of those debtors applied pressure upon Lord Ashe to get his money back?"

"When that happened, Lord Ashe turned to me."

"And you never denied him, or demanded repayment?"

"No, I did not."

"Why, then, did Lord Ashe give you the sugar plantation in Jamaica?"

John Collins looked from Theo Bryght over to where Lord Lauferby was standing. His look suggested he thought the Runner was more than a little mad. "Lord Lauferby, have you any idea what Mr. Bryght is talking about?"

"All right, then," said Theo Bryght. "What about this house? Why did Lord Ashe give it to you, if you were not pressuring him to repay you?"

"Again, to be frank, I do not know," replied Collins. "I suppose it was because a man has his pride, and so perhaps he wished to pay back at least a part of what he owed. But when I accepted Hopewell, I had no idea it would leave Lady Ashe without a home. I thought she was living at Ramblewood, Lord Ashe's estate. If I had known the truth, I would have insisted upon receiving that plantation in Curacao, or wherever you said it was located."

Theo Bryght stopped his questions and, instead, took several moments to study the man standing before him. "You puzzle me, Mr. Collins," he said, finally. "I do not mind admitting it. You puzzle me."

"Why is that, Mr. Bryght? I like to think I am plain-spoken man."

"That is just the trouble. I actually believe you. I do not think you would knowingly turn a young lady out of her home. Yet I do not believe Lord Lauferby ever paid you back. I think you returned those vowels to his purse when he was too drunk to notice. I also believe you did not pressure Lord Ashe to pay back the money he owed you. And that is why I am puzzled. Your words and actions proclaim you to be some sort of angel. Yet my eyes tell me you are a human being made out of flesh and blood. If I run a sword through you, you will not disappear into air, will you, Mr. Collins?"

"Are you mocking me?"

"No, but I would like to know why you are so generous. Why did you lend Lord Ashe such large sums of money?"

"That is easy to explain. When I returned to England, after I received my discharge from the army — I was wounded in Spain …"

"Yes, I heard something about that," replied Theo Bryght, glancing in the direction of the source of his information, Lord Lauferby. "Go on, what happened after you returned from England?"

"I wanted to buy into a small business, but I did not have enough money. I then remembered Lord Ashe, who had always been very kind to me in Spain, and asked if I could have a loan. That was before he began to gamble heavily, and he said he was happy to help me out — and I should come back to him if I were ever in a fix again."

"That was just the way he was, in the old days," said Lord Lauferby. "I can vouch for your story so far, Mr. Collins."

John Collins bowed slightly in the direction of the young lord, and then continued, saying, "And so I went into business, and my business was in the City, in London, and one day I was sitting in a coffee house when I overheard a conversation between two men who worked at the Stock Exchange. They were discussing what sounded like an exceptionally good investment. I started a conversation with them, and they told me that if I wanted to get in on the investment deal, too, I would have to buy my shares by the end of the week. I did not have the ready cash, since almost all of my capital was invested in my business, and so I returned to Lord Ashe. He gave me another loan. I invested the money in the Stock Exchange, and before I knew what had happened I had become a very, very wealthy man.

"It was like a dream. It still is like a dream," Collins continued. "I, of course, repaid Lord Ashe the money he had loaned me. But the amount seemed much too paltry for the good he had done me, since if he had not loaned me the money I would not have been able to invest it in those shares. And so when it was he who needed help, financially, I was only too glad to assist him."

"Would it not have been a greater kindness to encourage him to curb his gambling?" asked Theo Bryght.

"I often tried to talk to him, but he was not the sort of person who could be influenced. If I had not given him the money, he would have gotten it from a moneylender. And if he had done that, he would have been in even more serious trouble — I mean, financially. I never dreamed he would take his own life. I do not understand why he did not turn to me, if he was in such serious trouble."

Theo Bryght wanted to like John Collins. He admired working men who could maintain a sense of humanity in an often inhuman world. And he admired any poor devil born with a tin spoon in his mouth who somehow beat the odds and exchanged the tin for a silver one. But he distrusted too much goodness, just as he mistrusted people who professed to be entirely evil. And so he changed the subject and said, "Tell me about this mistress of Lord Ashe. She has red hair, I believe."

"I would not know."

"You never met her?"

Mr. Collins did not reply. Mr. Bryght waited. When the silence grew too long, Mr. Collins said, "Lord Ashe took me round to his clubs, because he needed me to pay his gambling debts. He had no need of me in the boudoir."

"A mistress can also be expensive. And gentlemen do talk."

"My father was in trade. I am not ashamed of that fact. My relationship with Lord Ashe was strictly financial."

Theo Bryght imagined this was probably true. A man like John Collins could have all the money in the world, yet he would never be accepted on equal footing by the *ton*. He therefore changed direction once again and said, "Have you a Bible in the room?"

"A Bible?"

"This is a library, and so I suppose there must be one," said Theo Bryght as he walked over to the shelves. "Yes, here is one." He opened the weighty volume and leafed through the pages. "Ah! Here it is: *'The wicked in his pride doth persecute the poor: let them be taken in the devices that they have imagined.'* Does that verse mean anything to you, Mr. Collins?"

"No, should it?"

"I thought that perhaps Lord Ashe might have mentioned it."

"I do not recall Lord Ashe quoting from the Bible."

"Yet a locket was found in the room where he died, and this verse was inscribed in the inside of the cover. Perhaps you saw the locket, or know of its significance?"

"If it is significant."

"You do not think it is, Mr. Collins?"

Mr. Collins shrugged and then gestured toward the room where they were standing. "And what if I were to die tomorrow? A colleague of yours would come snooping around the room and most likely find all kinds of interesting things. But they would have nothing to do with me, because they belonged to the former owner. Lord Ashe was living in rented rooms, Mr. Bryght. How can you be certain anything you found in that room belonged to him and not some earlier occupant?"

Theo Bryght did not reveal where the locket had been found. But once again he found himself puzzled by the former valet. John Collins was smart; there was no question about that. But was he also a liar, or was Theo

Bryght only displaying his class's prejudice when he found it interesting that the man had an answer for everything?

In the meanwhile, Collins had taken the Bible and put it back on its shelf. "You will excuse me ..."

Theo Bryght interrupted, saying, "Yes, the hour is getting on and you must be anxious to join Mrs. Collins in the dining room ..."

"I would prefer that you leave my wife out of this discussion."

The Runner and Lord Lauferby exchanged glances. At least they had found one thing out; there was a Mrs. Collins.

"Very well, but I was wondering if you could help me work through one last problem. It is something that has been puzzling me since I first became acquainted with the circumstances of Lord Ashe's death."

"If it can be stated briefly."

"I will do my best. You see, a Bow Street Runner likes death to be neat and tidy, and this death is not."

"Are you referring to the pen knife? Lady Ashe did mention something about it falling in the wrong place."

"Did she?"

"Lord Ashe was left-handed, as I am sure you have by now discovered, Mr. Bryght. One might therefore have thought the pen knife would have fallen beside his left foot, after he slit his right wrist. It was Lady Ashe's understanding, however, that the pen knife was found by his right foot. I, myself, cannot see what it matters where the knife fell, and so if this is the inconvenient detail you are referring to I cannot help solve your puzzle."

Theo Bryght tried not to smile. Inwardly, though, he thanked John Collins for the information he had just divulged. It had not occurred to him that the pen knife had fallen in the wrong place. This detail might turn out to be useful later on. For now, he said, "No, I was referring to something very different. I was referring to the fact that Lord Ashe was a soldier. He fought in the Peninsular Campaign, did he not, Mr. Collins?"

"Yes, he was in Spain."

"Did you have the opportunity to see Lord Ashe on the battlefield?"

"That is why we were sent to Spain, to fight the French."

"In your opinion, was Lord Ashe a brave soldier?"

"He was one of the best."

John Collins glanced over at Lord Lauferby, who chimed in, "I quite agree with you, Collins. I never saw a braver man when it came to fighting Boney's frogs."

"Good," Theo Bryght continued, "we have established that Lord Ashe showed courage on the battlefield. Would one not therefore expect him to display a similar courage when taking his own life — if he did, indeed, take his own life? That is still your opinion, is it not, Mr. Collins? You do still believe that Lord Ashe took his own life?"

"Yes, I do. But I do not understand the cause for your puzzlement."

"The weapon, Mr. Collins, the choice of weapon. A barber might slash his wrists, as might a poet, but not a soldier, not a soldier who was a gentleman. He would choose a more honourable weapon, such as a gun. Do you not see my point, Mr. Collins?"

"I see it."

"Yet you have nothing more to say?"

"What can I say, Mr. Bryght? How should I know what was in Lord Ashe's mind before he took his life? I am not a gentleman."

CANTO THE FIFTH

"Then you believe Collins did it?"

Lord Lauferby and Theo Bryght were back in the carriage, on their way to Lundsmoor Park. The Runner was trying to write, but the ruts in the country road were too much for the springs of even Lord Lauferby's expertly sprung carriage.

"I believe nothing of the sort," the Runner replied. "At least not yet."

"But the pen knife — you pressed him pretty hard about that."

"Because I wished to make a point, a point that had been bothering me for some time. I, myself, was never in the army, and so I can excuse myself for being squeamish when it comes to killing a man with a gun, especially when that man is oneself. But what do you think, Lauferby? Do you think Lord Ashe would have chosen a pen knife, when a gun would have done the job in an instant?"

"I never believed for a moment it was suicide."

"But if it were suicide? Would a former soldier choose such a death?"

"I cannot say, Bryght. There is something to be said for honour. But putting a gun to one's head ... think of the mess it would make to one's cravat!"

Theo Bryght laughed. "Thank you, Lauferby, that point escaped me entirely." The Runner then grew serious. "Of course, if Lord Ashe was murdered, it is the mind of the murderer that we must consider. I should think it would take more courage to slit another man's wrist, which would require personal contact, than to shoot him from a distance. The person who performed the crime would have had to be used to killing, whether that killing was done on the battlefield or in the alleyways of Brighton or London."

"Or in the sheepcotes of Yorkshire," said Lord Lauferby, looking gloomily out the window.

The Runner followed his glance. Their carriage was traveling through yet another green field heavily dotted with fluffs of white — the flocks of sheep that were as much a part of the Yorkshire moors as the mist and the ruts in the twisting roads. By this time next year, many of those sheep would have exchanged the moors for the serving platter, where they would be served up as leg of lamb or a mutton chop. Lauferby was right. Country life was only partially bucolic. It also had its violent side.

"Why are we going to see Lord March?" the young man persisted. "Do you think he might be the murderer?"

"And we are going to Lundsmoor Park like sheep to the slaughter?"

"I never did like Yorkshire very much."

"If you wish to return to Brighton, Lord Lauferby, I shall descend at the next town."

"No, I gave you my word," said Lauferby, showing a resolution the Runner had not guessed he possessed. "I stay until the final act."

II.

"It is the difference between night and day," said Mrs. Seymour, as she surveyed with approval the many platters of cakes and bowls of fruit that graced the long table in the drawing room.

Although Charlotte and Mrs. Seymour had not yet met Lady March, who had been unexpectedly called away to visit a sick tenant, this time Mrs. Seymour could find no fault with the reception that had been accorded to them. The servants of Lundsmoor Park had greeted them with a suitable show of respect upon their arrival, their rooms were excellent, and now they were being invited to sate their appetites on the delicacies that stood before them.

"I can only think that Lady March means to do you some good, Charlotte," Mrs. Seymour continued, carefully selecting a peach as she spoke. "Mark my words, one day you will recall this day as the day your fortune changed."

Charlotte tried to share her aunt's optimism. Yet as she gazed through the open window, which led on to a terrace that, in turn, gave way to a seemingly endless lawn, all she could feel was a certain pervasive numbness. She recalled an earlier walk she had taken on the Hopewell moors, when her disconnection from the land, from her home, had struck her with such force. And she wondered if this was how the rest of her life would always be — gazing through windows that were not hers at exquisite scenes that belonged to someone else.

She did not have time to linger with such thoughts, though, since Lady March had entered the room. The usual civilities must be exchanged: the gracious invitation must be acknowledged, the handsome rooms must be admired; concern for the ill tenant must be expressed; the ensuing awkward silence must somehow be bridged.

When all this had been accomplished, Lady March suggested that her two guests accompany her on a tour of the grounds — if, of course, Mrs. Seymour was not too tired from the journey and preferred to rest. Mrs. Seymour, rising to the occasion with admirable alacrity, insisted she must really have her rest before dinner. And so after that good lady had retired to her room, which fortunately afforded an excellent view of at least part of the lawn, Charlotte accompanied Lady March outside.

It was a sultry day, suggesting that a thunderstorm might make an appearance during the evening. Yet despite the heat, Charlotte had to admit the grounds were lovely. Although the lawn had been cleared many years ago of the dense forest that gave Lundsmoor Park its name — the Park had once been the exclusive hunting grounds of English kings — this forest could be quickly reached by the many paths that wandered off the wide swath of well-kept green. Thus the pleasing representation of all that was civilized and tame was saved from tedium by the ever-present sense of a world that was natural and wild.

In the distance was a small enclosed domed building, a *faux* Doric Temple, which Charlotte rightly guessed was their destination. When they entered she was charmed to see that the walls had all been painted with a series of pastoral scenes. The style was one which reflected the sensibility of an earlier time and the paintwork suggested the hand of one who still young and inexpert, and yet it was all done with such evident love and joy that the room fairly glowed with happiness and good will.

"It is lovely," said Charlotte. "You must enjoy coming here very much."

"In truth, I do not come here very often. For me, the memories are bittersweet. I painted these scenes when I was young, and ..."

"You painted them?" Charlotte could not help but blurt out.

Lady March did not appear to be offended. "Yes, Lady Ashe, I too was once young. I know it is the way of the world to assume an older person was always uninteresting, but that is only because we do not take the time to truly see a person and inquire what lies below the surface."

"I only meant to say, Ma'am, I am surprised you had time, when you were already a wife and mother, to complete such an ambitious project."

"I completed it before I was married. I came to Lundsmoor Park as an orphan, Lady Ashe, and so you see we have something else in common, in addition to our enjoyment of art. I know what it is to be alone in the world, without the benefit of a mother's love and a father's guidance. Of course, our situations were not entirely similar. My marriage to my future husband had already been arranged. I came to this place knowing that one day I would be its mistress."

"You must love it very much."

"I do. Yet as a person gets older, one is less concerned about the carpets and the silver. It is people that interests one, which is why I have invited you here."

"I am flattered by your interest, Lady March, but I cannot imagine what I have done to warrant such concern," replied Charlotte as her heart began to sink. She offered a silent prayer that the beautiful scene would not be forever marred by the mention of a position for a governess that had become available.

"For one thing, you have lost fifty thousand pounds on a bad bet," replied Lady March, "and losing a fortune is always of interest in my circle. For another, you have refused my offer of financial assistance, which was an act of either great strength of character or total recklessness. As you have not been wrecked by your misfortunes, I can therefore safely presume you are a person worth knowing. Finally, you are young. You should be married and surrounded by your children. With your permission, I shall take steps to do what I can to bring you to this blessed, happy state."

Charlotte stared, too shocked to speak. She could not imagine what sort of husband Lady March had in mind, but she assumed it was a tenant farmer or some other man of that ilk. The thought of having to live on Lady March's land and be eternally grateful to her for this supposed kindness made Charlotte feel ill.

But before she could speak, Lady March continued, saying, "I do not wish you to be under any misapprehensions while you are here. If my son, Lord March, should pay you certain attentions during your stay, you have my permission to return them. I should not mind if you were to be the mistress of Lundsmoor Park in my place."

"I do not understand," Charlotte replied, this new shock having stunned her into speech. "If you are trifling with me, Lady March, teasing me to see if I am some female fortune hunter for your own sport and amusement, I must ask your permission to return to Butterhill at once."

"I am perfectly serious, Lady Ashe. If you can win my son's heart, Lundsmoor Park is yours."

"But why? I have no fortune. You know that better than anyone."

"True, but you do have something I want."

"What is that?"

"Good sense. Integrity. A sense of self worth. If you can give me grandchildren who possess those same qualities — grandchildren who are not simpering imbeciles — I shall consider myself the winner of this argument."

Lady March then added, "When I first came to Lundsmoor Park, it was full of life. I would like to see it full of life again, before I leave it."

III.

Charlotte longed to talk with someone, and yet she did not feel able to reveal to Mrs. Seymour all that had been spoken in the Doric Temple. Mrs. Seymour did not know about her feelings for John Collins, nor would she be able to understand how feelings for a married man might hinder Charlotte from considering a proposal of marriage from Lord March favorably.

"But my thoughts are running too far ahead," she murmured as she gazed into the mirror.

"My lady?" asked Ella, who was arranging Charlotte's hair.

"Are these curls too close to my head?" said Charlotte, returning her attention to the business of dressing for dinner.

"It is the weather, my lady. The air is very damp."

A few minutes later Charlotte's toilette was completed and she went down to the drawing room. She was surprised to see that Lord and Lady Cunningham were there, as was Odelia, who was seated at the pianoforte, playing one of the sad and yearning melodies that her nature seemed to favor. Mrs. Seymour had been given a chair next to Lady March, while Lord March sat at a writing table, writing and seemingly oblivious to them all — although he did look up when Charlotte entered the room.

"Lord and Lady Cunningham have surprised us with a visit," Lady March said to Charlotte, while gesturing to Charlotte to take a seat on the sofa beside her. "I thought they might have come to pay their respects to you, Lady Ashe, but they assure me most vehemently they had not heard you were staying at Lundsmoor Park."

Lord and Lady Cunningham exchanged uncomfortable glances. Charlotte noticed that Lady March was enjoying their discomfort immensely, and she soon discovered the reason why.

"You will be taking Odelia to London next year for the season?" Lady March asked them.

"If she is not married before then," Lady Cunningham replied, with an attempt at a smile.

"I cannot imagine who she will find to marry, cooped up as she is all the time at Ramblewood. I suppose there is Lord Randolph's eldest son, but the estate is much diminished."

"Sadly diminished," said Lady Cunningham, refusing to be riled by the mention of Lord Randolph and that gentleman's eldest son, who was commonly considered to be lacking in even the most basic social graces. "It is nothing like Lundsmoor Park, or Ramblewood. We are all so very fond of Ramblewood."

"It will be a pity, then, when you will be forced to leave it."

Lady Cunningham's face turned pale. Odelia stopped her playing in mid-phrase and turned to stare at Lady March. Even Lord March stopped his writing and stared at his mother. It was Lord Cunningham, though, who retained the presence of mind to speak.

"What exactly do you mean, Lady March? Has the estate been confiscated by the Crown, after all? Or must it be sold?"

"I assure you, Lord Cunningham, I have heard no news," replied Lady March with an innocent smile. "I was merely expressing an opinion that a person should not become too attached to a place they will one day be forced to leave."

At dinner Lady March proved to be a lively conversationalist, although Charlotte wished, for Odelia's sake, that the elder woman would have refrained from her many mentions of the necessity of sending the girl to London to find a husband. It was a relief to almost everyone when the butler announced the unexpected arrival of two visitors.

"At this hour?" asked Lady March. "Who are they?"

"A Lord Lauferby, Ma'am, and a Mister Theo Bryght," replied the butler.

When Lady March shot an inquiring glance over at her son, Lord March said, "The Bow Street Runner from London."

IV.

"I am surprised at March," said Lord Lauferby, gazing gloomily at his plate of cold meat, "giving you the brush off like you were a brother of the whip."

"I was perfectly content to have my supper in the kitchen, so you could join the others in the dining room, my lord," replied Theo Bryght.

Lauferby scowled at his dinner companion. "If you would only let me tell the Dowager who you really are."

"Hush! I am a Bow Street Runner. A plate of cold meat and a tankard of ale served in the third-best sitting room of a country manor suits me fine."

Their conversation was interrupted by the entrance of the butler, who informed them that Lady March and her guests had retired to the drawing room. Theo Bryght and Lord Lauferby followed the butler down the long hall and into the brightly lit room.

Introductions were made. The Runner noted the presence of Lady March and Lord and Lady Cunningham and their daughter, all of whom he was meeting for the first time. But his gaze kept returning to Lady Ashe. He thought she looked particularly lovely.

"Have you news for us, Mr. Bryght?" asked Lady March, after the introductions were over.

"I have come to impose upon your hospitality, Ma'am," said the Runner with all the assumed deference he could muster. "There are several people sitting in this room who I must speak to, but it is not a task I can accomplish in one night."

Lady March was not pleased with this intrusion into the little matrimonial drama she had so carefully prepared, but the Runner's request was granted. After the Runner received assurances that the Cunnighams had no intention of leaving Ramblewood, they were allowed to return home. The ladies were also allowed to retire to their rooms. It was Lord March who the Runner wished to speak with first, and so after Lord Lauferby made a reluctant exit it was they who were left in the room.

Lord March poured out two glasses of wine and gave one to Theo Bryght. Then he said, "It is late, Mr. Bryght. Shall we come straight to the point?"

"With pleasure, my lord," Theo Bryght said, while removing the diary from his coat pocket. "Do you recognize this?"

"No. Should I?"

"It is a diary. It belonged to Lord Ashe. Your name appears in it once. Shall I tell you when?"

Lord March gazed down at the wine in his glass. "There is no need. I remember the time very well."

"Yet not well enough to inform me of it when you were in Brighton, is that not so? You could have saved me a very long journey."

"Is the appointment so very important?"

"That depends."

"On what?"

"On whether Lord Ashe left the appointment dead or alive."

"You are forgetting that there is a third possibility, Mr. Bryght."

"Which is?"

"That Lord Ashe never came."

Theo Bryght took a sip of the wine in his glass. It was an excellent vintage — strong, too — and for a moment he was tempted to down the entire glass in one long drink. Perhaps he would have more luck with solving this murder if he were drunk.

Instead, he placed the glass on the table and said, "That is your story? Lord Ashe never showed up for this appointment?"

"Yes."

"Very well, but I am a curious man. Please tell me about this appointment that did not take place."

"There is not much to tell. I received a note from Ashe the morning before he died. He informed me he would be fighting a duel that night, and he asked me to be his second. He said he would send a carriage for me at two o'clock in the morning. The carriage never came."

"You did not go to his rooms to inquire for him?"

"Not at that hour." Lord March then added, "If he had been staying in his own residence, one would feel no qualms about waking the servants. But he was staying in rented rooms."

Theo Bryght could see that. Lord March was not the type to willingly make a spectacle in a public street in the middle of the night, something that might happen if the servants of the house were particularly sound sleepers. His next question therefore took another direction: "Did it not strike you odd that Lord Ashe should ask you to be his second? I understand your relations were strained."

"I was surprised, I will admit."

"Yet you agreed?"

"Yes."

"In writing?"

Lord March hesitated, and then their eyes met. It was clear they were both considering the same fact: No letter from Lord March was found in the Brighton room where Lord Ashe had died.

"Did Lord Ashe mention what this duel was about?" asked Theo Bryght, again changing direction.

"He wrote that he would explain in the carriage."

"You were not curious? You did not attempt to see him in the afternoon?"

"I had other engagements."

"Which were more important than trying to talk him out of this foolishness?"

"I thought there would be time to speak in the carriage. It is not unheard of for two gentlemen with a quarrel to reach a satisfactory agreement at the last hour."

Theo Bryght remained silent, while he tried to piece together the events of Lord Ashe's final night on earth. The man had dressed for dinner, with the help of the parlour maid. He had looked ill, in the girl's opinion. Perhaps he had been, or perhaps he had been afraid. He had then gone to Lord Lauferby's to dine, where, in Lauferby's opinion, he had looked worried. So far, Lord March's story seemed plausible. A man, on the eve of a duel, might look ill and worried. But then what happened?

Lord Ashe went with the members of the dinner party — which included John Collins — to the gaming establishment. Had John Collins mentioned anything about Lord Ashe's health or appearance? The Runner could not remember for certain, but he thought not. Was that important? He did not know.

And then what happened? They gambled. They drank. Lord Lauferby landed under the table. Lord Ashe left, either alone or accompanied by other members of his party. His diary slipped from his pocket and landed on the pavement outside the front door of the gaming establishment. How did that happen? Did the young man trip on a step, which loosened the small volume from his coat pocket? Did someone push him? If only someone had seen Lord Ashe leave!

And then what happened? Did Lord Ashe walk to his rooms? Did he take a carriage? Another blank. Apparently no one in the house heard him enter, or climb the stairs, or enter his rooms. And then what happened? He sat down at the table? He took pen and ink from the writing box? It could have happened that way. What could be more natural, on what was possibly the last night of one's life, than to write a letter, a letter of farewell to one's wife and family, a letter of instruction to one's solicitor? But if that was the case, why was there no letter, no blotting paper? Why were there only the pen, the ink, and the pen knife?

And then what happened? Another blank.

He therefore asked, "And then what happened, Lord March?"

"I went to bed."

"I was referring to Lord Ashe. Have you an opinion?"

"It is my opinion Lord Ashe lost his nerve and took his life."

"A man who had fought in Spain?"

"It was my understanding that Lord Ashe, upon his return to England, was a changed man."

"Because?"

Lord March shook his head. "He did not confide in me."

"And so to prevent Ramblewood from being confiscated by the Crown, you returned to Lord Ashe's rooms, after the initial discovery of the body, and removed the letter you had written agreeing to be his second. You also disturbed the clothes, so it would look like there had been a murder and the murderer had returned. Is that correct?"

"Yes. But it was not only to save Ramblewood. You may choose to believe me or not, as you please, Mr. Bryght, but my first thought was to spare Lord Ashe's widow and our family unnecessary pain."

V.

When Theo Bryght arrived in the breakfast room the following morning he was not sure if he had arrived too early or too late. The buffet table was groaning under the weight of heavy silver serving platters filled with eggs and meat and whatever else a person could wish to fill his stomach with. But other than the servants the room was empty.

He noticed that the door to the terrace was open, and he walked outside. The air had cleared after an early morning rain and the lawn was a dazzling green. After living so many years in the crowded, noisy streets of London, the sight of so much green and quiet beckoned to him and he followed its call. He was soon tempted to follow one of the wooded paths, and he wandered contentedly, thinking of nothing except the singing of the birds and the rustling of the leaves.

The path eventually wound its way back to the lawn, and there he saw them: Lord March and Lady Ashe. They were apparently taking a leisurely early morning stroll and were as startled to see him as he was to see them. He bowed in their direction, and again took note of Lady Ashe's appearance. Even in mourning clothes she was an uncommonly attractive woman; white muslin would make her look like an angel.

Lord March and Lady Ashe bowed stiffly in his direction and continued with their walk. The Runner looked after them. They made a fine-looking couple. Provided that Lord March was not a murderer, of course, it would be a fine match for Lady Ashe. She could do worse than marry a rich peer of the realm, much worse. She could marry someone like him, a Bow Street Runner living in rented rooms in London, for example.

VI.

Eventually the party did assemble for breakfast. The Cunninghams arrived during the meal and the Runner interviewed Lord Cunningham first.

"Did Lord Ashe have any enemies, sir?"

"None that I know of."

"Did Lord Ashe ever ask you for money, to pay off his gambling debts?"

"No, he did not."

Theo Bryght was not surprised. If he had been in trouble, Lord Cunningham was the last person he would have turned to, as well. The man was too insufferably dull and smug by half. But to satisfy his conscience that he had done his duty, the Runner asked one more question:

"Did Lord Ashe ever talk to you about Spain?"

"Spain?" The former soldier's eyes lit up.

"I believe an incident occurred involving a local girl."

The lights went out. "I cannot see what that has to do with anything, Mr. Bryght."

"There have been some attempts at blackmail," said the Runner, being purposely vague. Lord Cunningham did not have to know that he was referring to the letters received by Lord Lauferby and John Collins.

"Blackmail?" Lord Cunningham considered this for a few minutes, and then he said, "That puts things in a different light. Do you think that was it? Ashe was being blackmailed?"

"It is a possibility, sir," the Runner replied. For what if Lord Lauferby had been right? What if someone were trying to extort money from the group that had been in Spain? But why? What had happened there that was so heinous it could frighten an Englishman who was a peer of the realm and therefore, in most instances, above the law?

"What happened in Spain?" Bryght asked a second time.

"There was something about a young woman. I believe she came from a reasonably prosperous, respectable family," said Lord Cunningham. "But she was not a member of the Spanish aristocracy, by any means."

"Did Lord Ashe wish to marry the lady?"

"Good lord, no! It was just a harmless flirtation."

Theo Bryght did not say what he was thinking, that the flirtation had been far from harmless for the girl. Or that it might have turned out to be more dangerous for

Lord Ashe than anyone could have possible expected. Instead, he asked, "Was there contact between Lord Ashe and the young woman after he returned to England?"

"There was, now that I recall it. Or rather it was the girl's brother who wrote. Lord Ashe showed me the letter. It was written in a funny sort of English, but then the man was a foreigner."

"And what did the letter say?"

"That the girl had been left in the family way and the family desired payment. They regarded it as a sort of debt of honour. Lord Ashe showed me the letter because he was not sure what he should do."

"Did you advise him to pay the money?"

"Absolutely not!" exclaimed Lord Cunningham. "I do not wish to sound uncaring, Bryght, but I told Lord Ashe not to be a fool. Who was to say the child was really his? And once you give people like that some money, they will come back for more again and again. There will be no end to it. 'Burn the letter,' I told him. 'Let them play their Spanish tricks somewhere else.'"

"Did he take your advice?"

"I hope so, but I do not know. I can tell you, though, that he never mentioned the incident again."

The interview with Lady Cunningham was brief. She knew nothing of her brother's affairs and Theo Bryght had no interest in listening to her complaints concerning Lady Ashe. He therefore escorted her out of the room as quickly as he could.

Lady Ashe, herself, was the next person to enter the room, and the Runner did his best to keep his thoughts on the business that had brought him to Lundsmoor Park. After he was informed of the letter she had sent to Brighton — and made a mental note that missing letters seemed to be a distinguishing feature of this crime — he informed her of his interview with John Collins.

Although he was by this point inclined to view Lord Ashe's death as suicide, he was in no hurry to bring *this* interview to a close. He therefore said, "Mr. Collins mentioned something about the pen knife being found in the wrong place. This concerns you?"

"My husband was left-handed. If the knife fell from his left hand, would it not have been more natural for it to have fallen by his left side?"

"That would be expected. But we cannot always know how the body will react, when it is in the throes of death. Perhaps his arm jerked and the knife was thrown to the other side."

As there was nothing more to discuss, he let her leave him.

VII.

Theo Bryght spent the afternoon in his room. As far as he was concerned, his inquiry had come to a close. But to make sure he was satisfied with how he had tidied all the loose ends, he put down his thoughts in writing.

First he described the victim and the events of Lord Ashe's final day. Next he considered his list of suspects and their motives:

Lord Lauferby had wanted to borrow money from John Collins, who was Lord Ashe's "banker." Lord Ashe had not been happy to possibly lose the services of Mr. Collins, whose funds, while ample, were not limitless. Had the two young men quarreled, and had the quarrel turned violent? It was unlikely, and so the Runner left Lord Lauferby under the table of the gaming establishment, sleeping away the night.

Lord March had suffered a supposed insult to his honour in Spain, which caused a break in his relations with Lord Ashe. Lord March also stood to inherit Ramblewood, should Lord Ashe die without issue, which is what happened. An illegitimate child born in Spain would not alter the lines of inheritance. But unless Lord March was an uncommonly vengeful and greedy man, it was doubtful he would murder his cousin. And so even though the story about the duel was not entirely satisfactory, one could say there is very little in life that is entirely satisfactory and so it is therefore unrealistic to expect a person's story to be without flaw.

Lord and Lady Cunningham were insufferable snobs, but he doubted they would wish any harm to Lord Ashe since they had nothing to gain by his death. They were comfortably settled on Lord Ashe's estate, they but could remain only so long as he was alive.

John Collins was an easy man to suspect. His goodness, his loyalty, his story of unexpected good fortune and virtue rewarded and all that — Theo Bryght did not mind admitting he despised the man. But not because he thought John Collins was a murderer. There was no proof John Collins had accompanied Lord Ashe to his rooms, after their evening of gambling. The halo must remain firmly in place.

He supposed he did have to include Lady Ashe in his list, and so the Runner dipped his pen into the inkwell and continued to write. If anyone had reason to murder her husband, Theo Bryght thought it was Lady Ashe. Lord Ashe had squandered her fortune. He had very likely betrayed her with another woman. Yet she would accomplish very little by the act. Without a fortune, she could not have expected to marry again. If she were to marry Lord March, it would be a stroke of luck and not something she could have planned — unless they had planned the murder together. He kept coming back to that — and rejecting it. There was no passion between Lady Ashe and Lord March. He had noticed that. If they were to marry it would be one of those very proper, very respectable, very dull arrangements. Lord March would provide the land and the wealth, she would provide the heir. Long live England.

That left the Runner with just one other person: the Spanish lady's brother. If there really had been a duel planned, the only logical second party was this mysterious man. Had the man come to Lord Ashe's rooms before the duel, which led to a quarrel, which led to the man killing Lord Ashe with the pen knife?

It broke all the rules of dueling, of course, to meet before the duel. Using pen knives as the choice of weapon would also be frowned upon. But at least this was a story one could chew on. And so the Runner allowed himself the luxury of conjuring up an image of this mysterious Spaniard. He would be dark, of course, and hot-tempered. The fire of the insult to his sister had probably been extinguished long ago; perhaps by now the girl was even dead. But the money — assuming Lord Ashe was paying him money — that would keep the sting of an insult to the family honour burning bright. And if for some reason Lord Ashe had insisted on stopping the payments …

Theo Bryght stopped writing. Although he, himself, did not entirely believe in the existence of this greedy Spanish brother, he felt he had at last arrived at a motive worth killing for. If Lord Ashe had allowed himself to be blackmailed — by somebody, anybody — and now he wished to stop the payments — perhaps because he had exhausted his resources, including those of John Collins — there was every reason to believe the blackmailer would threaten Lord Ashe. And once angry words were exchanged it would be only a matter of time before the quarrel turned violent.

But who was the blackmailer? Who needed money badly enough that he would kill to get it?

And then it struck him. The blackmail may have been about money, but it did not necessarily follow that the blackmailer needed the money. It could be done for the pure enjoyment of torturing another human being — and watching that person tumble into an abyss of fear and despair.

He glanced over his list of suspects a second time, and two names stared back at him. But which one was his man?

VIII.

"I do not mind eating in the sitting room, Bryght. Truly I do not care."

"Just because I have been banished to that uncomfortable, uncertain realm of tenants and tradesmen does not mean your stomach should suffer, Lauferby. I shall eat supper in my room and spare us all the agony of this socially awkward situation."

Lord Lauferby made a few more protestations and then disappeared down the stairs. Theo Bryght returned to his room, but he did not close his door completely. There was another reason why he had chosen to sup upstairs on this night.

After he heard the last of the party descend using the front stairs, and heard their servants descend to their quarters using the back stairs, he quietly made his way to Lord March's room. He hoped the man kept his correspondence there, and not in the library. Although Lundsmoor Park was large it was too well staffed to make creeping about the public rooms a comfortable experience.

As he had hoped, a secretary stood in Lord March's private sitting room. The Runner ignored the unlocked drawers and fixed his attention, instead, upon a generous sized locked compartment that looked promising. The lock was no challenge to his skilled fingers, but the moment of triumph proved to be fleeting. All he found were tenants' leases and other papers concerning the management of Lord March's estate. But though he might be disappointed he was not devastated. He still had time. Supper in the Lundsmoor Park dining hall was a lavish affair, and Theo Bryght assumed they were still sipping their soup.

He therefore turned his eye to a smaller compartment and his hand to fiddling with what had proven to be a finicky lock.

"Is this what you are looking for?"

Theo Bryght felt the skin on the back of his neck start to prickle. When given a choice, he really did prefer to break into another person's room in peace and quiet. The experience of being caught in the act, when it occurred, was invariably unpleasant. And so as he slowly turned to face his unexpected questioner, he could only think, "Blast this murder!"

CANTO THE SIXTH

Theo Bryght would have preferred to travel to Whitby alone, and in the carriage of Lord Lauferby. Instead, he found himself in the company of a large party that was comprised of too many carriages and characterized by too much conversation.

Three of the ladies — Lady March, Lady Ashe, and Mrs. Seymour — were in one carriage, which was perhaps the happiest one of the caravan. During the past several days Lady March and Mrs. Seymour had discovered a mutual interest in homemade remedies, and so they spent the hours of travel engaged in happy consultation, discussing the merits of the various flowers and herbs and grasses that they passed.

The Cunninghams traveled in their own barouche, although Lord Cunningham did not seem at all happy about this unnecessary use of his horses. Lady Cunningham looked merely determined to be one of any party that included Lady Ashe. That left the Runner to watch the scenery in the presence of Lord Lauferby and Lord March, who were conversing about horses, hunting, and other country topics.

When they reached Whitby, the Runner alighted from his carriage near the entrance to the town, while the others proceeded in the direction of the old Abbey. A few moments later the Runner was seated across from Lady Ashe's solicitor, Mr. Inkerwell, who was saying, "This is very irregular, Mr. ..."

"Bryght. Theo Bryght. You may send to London if you do not believe I am a Bow Street Runner. I believe there is a mail coach leaving within the hour. But it is my opinion Lady Ashe may be in some danger, and so I should be sorry for the delay."

Mr. Inkerwell again studied the man's papers. When he was finally satisfied he had done all he could, under the circumstances, to ascertain that the man really was who he said he was, Mr. Inkerwell went to his locked cupboard and opened it.

"I examined the transfer of ownership of Hopewell to Mr. Collins very carefully," the solicitor said, as he handed a piece of paper to the Runner. 'This is a copy. The original is, I presume, in the possession of Mr. Collins."

"Were you familiar with Lord Ashe's handwriting?"

"No, but ..." Mr. Inkerwell had not had occasion to blush for many years, but he did blush now. "The state of Lord Ashe's affairs was abominable," he continued. "Gambling debts, debts to tradesmen — there was no end to them. And they all proved to be authentic. I had no reason to suspect this one piece of paper was forged."

Theo Bryght nodded his head. For the moment he was too busy reading to do anything more.

It was a clever piece of work, if it was, indeed, a forgery. Yet how had the forger had access to the original letter, which had been mailed earlier in the day?

"The blotting paper!" he cried out, to the extreme surprise of Mr. Inkerwell.

He did not care if Mr. Inkerwell thought he had gone insane. He had no time to explain to the solicitor that if the paper used to blot the ink of the original document had been lying on Lord Ashe's desk — and if the forger had found it — the man could have used the blotting paper as his guide for copying Lord Ashe's handwriting and signature. The man had only to change the name of the new owner of Hopewell and the deed was done. Should the possessor of the original document protest it would be his word against the word of the other. The two documents were so alike it would be nigh impossible to say which of them was true and which was false.

But if one of the two men was also a murderer, the scales of justice must tip in favor of the other.

Theo Bryght took the original letter from his coat pocket and thrust it into the solicitor's hands. "Guard this paper with your life, Mr. Inkerwell! Do not show it to anyone until I return.

"Mr. Bryght?"

Both Theo Bryght and Mr. Inkerwell turned toward the doorway, where the solicitor's assistant was standing.

"There has been an accident, sir, at the Abbey. You are asked to come at once."

II.

Although Theo Bryght was a Runner, he could not recall ever running as quickly as that day when he ran through the narrow streets of Whitby, shoving his way through the crowds of people and carts, and leaping up the almost two hundred steps that led to the top of the hill where the Abbey stood.

Standing atop the hill was a small crowd of people huddled together in what had once been sacred space. He continued to push forward, and then he saw it: a woman, dressed in black, her lifeless body lying on the ground.

When he reached her, he kneeled down upon the ground and stretched out his hand to touch the back of the woman's head, which was veiled. He then gently turned the woman's face toward him.

What he saw gave him a start.

"Who is she?" he asked, glancing wildly at the crowd. It was only then that he noticed the ladies from Lundsmoor Park standing off to the side, away from the gaggle of curious onlookers. It was only then, when he saw Lady Ashe standing with them, that he felt his heart return to its normal pace.

He returned his attention to the lifeless woman in his arms. A dagger had been thrust into her heart. One hand still clutched its hilt.

"Who is she?" he demanded a second time.

Still no one answered. The crowd, which included Lauferby and March and, strangely, John Collins, as well, stood staring at the dead woman as though they had all been turned to stone. He therefore cried out yet a third time, "For God's sake, can no one tell me who this unfortunate woman is?"

"She is my wife."

The Runner stared at John Collins, but before he could say anything Lord March had stepped forward and demanded, "Your *wife*?"

"Yes, my wife," John Collins replied, casting a dark glance in Lord March's direction. He then said to the Runner, "Will you help me move her body to a more fitting place?"

While arrangements were being made to transport the body, Theo Bryght noticed that Lord March could not take his eyes off the dead woman's face. The Runner nodded his question to Lord Lauferby, who mouthed a one-word reply: Spain.

III.

"We were on our way to London. I had recently learned of a medical man there who claimed he had cured many diseases of the mind. I had a hope he would be able to cure my wife, as well."

John Collins took a sip of his wine. Theo Bryght hated to press a man whose wife had just died, but he had no choice.

"Did you know your wife was ill when you married her?" he asked.

"She was not ill when I married her. That happened after her child died."

"*Her* child?"

"I thought by now you would have heard the entire story, Mr. Bryght."

"Apparently there are others who did not know the lady was married to you."

John Collins smiled a grim smile. "No, I suppose that did come as a shock to Lord March. But I can tell you that she never cared for him, even though he was besotted with her. It was Lord Ashe that she foolishly gave her heart to."

"He did not return the sentiment?"

"Oh, he was happy enough to make love to her while he was in Spain. But when he returned to England he forgot all about her, even though she was carrying his child."

"And you married her, knowing all this?"

"I was wounded more severely than the others, and so I had to stay behind. I could see she was desperately unhappy. I therefore thought I could do some good in the world, if I married her. No one would have to know the child was not mine, especially if we returned to England. And she was very lovely. She was the most beautiful woman I had ever seen."

"Why do you insist it was suicide, Mr. Collins? Perhaps it was a common thief that killed her."

"No. It was my dagger. I got it in Spain. She must have taken it from my cupboard before we left Hopewell and packed it with her things. I shall never forgive that woman Maria for leaving my wife unattended. Never!"

IV.

Theo Bryght left the bereaved husband to mourn and went to the inn where the party from Lundsmoor Park had reserved their own sitting room. The Runner had asked that no one leave Whitby without his permission.

He noticed at once that Lady Ashe was not in the room. Upon questioning it became clear that no one knew where she had gone. Mrs. Seymour had felt faint and retired to one of the inn's bedrooms. Lady March had busied herself with preparing a remedy for fainting spells that was of her own device, and she had sent Lady Cunningham and Odelia to the apothecary's shop for ingredients. Lord March was also absent, although no one knew where he had gone. That left Lord Cunningham and Lord Lauferby, who had quickly discovered they had absolutely nothing in common. They therefore sat in silence, each with his glass of his wine and his thoughts.

The Runner went back outside, in search of Lady Ashe. Whitby was not a large metropolis like London, but it was not a one-street village either. And so after ascertaining that she was not strolling down one of the streets lined with shops, he walked to the pier, which stood before him in all its English seafaring glory. A ship was being outfitted for a journey and the calls of the porters and the ship's mates sang through the air. A group of people was watching the loading of the vessel with interest, but Lady Ashe was not among them. He therefore turned away from the busy scene, almost poignant in its everyday normalcy, and followed the shoreline in the direction of the East Cliff.

He wished he could find Lady Ashe. He was concerned for her safety, of course, but he was also sorry about what had happened to Mrs. Collins and he wanted to say that to someone other than the gulls. He also wanted to say he was sorry that people for some reason kept falling in love with people who did not return their love, but that was something he could not say to Lady Ashe, even if he did find her.

The further he walked, the wilder the shore became. He surmised that this was where the smugglers landed their vessels, in the middle of the night, or where lovers came to secretly meet. Clambering over the rocky shore, he rounded a portion of the cliff wall that jutted out toward the sea. And then he saw her, in the distance, seated upon a rocky ledge, and even though he had been looking for Lady Ashe all this time he was still surprised to find her. For a moment he allowed himself the pleasure of indulging in the fantasy that she was waiting for him. But he knew it could not be so. Yet why was she there — and there alone?

He found a place behind a boulder where he could observe her without being observed and waited. When he realized the waves were gathering strength and would soon prevent him from overhearing any conversation that might occur, he gave up his hiding place and found one that was closer, but which offered a lesser view.

Lady Ashe was staring out to sea, which seemed to be a perfectly normal thing to do after the shock of the afternoon. Yet she was clearly waiting for someone. Every few minutes she turned her head in the direction of the town, as though she expected to see someone approaching. The Runner followed her gaze.

They both heard the sound of the footsteps at the same time. The Runner knew those footsteps must belong to either one of two men: Lord March or John Collins. One of them was a blackmailer and a murderer, and in the back of his mind the Runner was standing in some gambling hell, where the dealer was smiling at the assembled players and saying, "Gentlemen, place your bets."

In an instant, the play was over. John Collins stopped when he saw Lady Ashe, and the Runner hoped she would not go towards him, which would ruin everything. She stayed where she was, and it was Collins who walked the rest of the way.

"You should not have sent for me, Lady Ashe. I warned you at Hopewell. Your reputation ..."

"Your concern for my reputation is touching, Mr. Collins, especially after this."

The Runner saw that she had shoved a piece of paper into Collins's hand, and he groaned when he saw the broken seal. That fool of a solicitor had disobeyed his orders and apparently given the original letter to Lady Ashe.

"Lord Ashe never gave you Hopewell, not as a gift and not as a bribe. He transferred ownership of Hopewell to Lord March, to protect himself from the person who was blackmailing him. And that person was you, Mr. Collins. You forged the paper you showed to Mr. Inkerwell. Can you deny it?"

"I could Lady Ashe. I could say the document giving me ownership is the true one, and that it is Lord March who forged that other paper. But I daresay you would not believe me. Lord March is a peer of the realm, and I am only a former valet."

The Runner could see that Lady Ashe hesitated, and he did not blame her. He had been puzzling through the problem of the two letters ever since the night when Odelia Cunnigham had discovered him breaking into Lord March's room. It was she who had given him the letter from Lord Ashe, which transferred ownership of Hopewell to Lord March.

Which was the true document and which was the one that was false? Which of the two men was the blackmailer who, if not an actual murderer, had destroyed the life of the young lord just the same? He hoped Lady Ashe would guess correctly, for her sake, as well as for his.

"If only I could believe you," Lady Ashe finally said. "But why would Lord March care about Hopewell, when he has so much? It makes no sense."

"I have often asked myself a similar question," John Collins replied with a slight smile. "Why is it that noblemen like Lord March, and your late husband, who have so much, why is it that they must play with the lives of the poor and destroy them? You look puzzled, Lady Ashe. Let me explain what I mean. I had a sister who was even more beautiful than you. But she had the misfortune to be just a simple serving girl in a Whitby inn. She gave herself to the younger son of some earl, or perhaps it was a baronet. But whoever it was, he took his pleasure and threw her away when he was done. If you would like to visit my sister, Lady Ashe, go up the hill to the cemetery. You will find her there, in a place which is reserved for young girls who have taken their lives, after those lives were destroyed by the 'My Lords' of the world. You will recognize her resting place. It is the one with the headstone that says, 'Psalm Ten, Verse Two'."

"The locket?"

"So you do know about the locket. I thought so. If you have it, perhaps you will do me the favor of returning it to me? I only lent it to your husband, as a memento from Spain. It was not his — or yours — to keep."

Charlotte removed the locket from a pocket in her pelisse and handed it to him. "You may have it, Mr. Collins, with my compliments. I do not want it. But I still do not understand what this has to do with my husband. He did not betray your sister."

"No, but to me one "My Lord" is very much like another. I therefore chose Lord Ashe to be the man on whom I would take my revenge, both for my sister and for myself. You see, I married the girl who your husband had used and thrown away in Spain. But instead of thanking me for it, she despised me. Why? Because she was still in love with your husband, Lady Ashe, even after what he had done. And so after I made my fortune, I decided to make sport of your husband, for my amusement. I invented a brother for my dear wife, who soon learned to regret her contempt for me. I invented a dangerous, hot-tempered Spaniard who was anxious to avenge the family honour, which could only be done through the transfer of large sums of money into his pocket. This locket, with its charming curl of my wife's hair, was the brother's initial calling card. Oh, I cannot tell you how I inwardly laughed, Lady Ashe, when your husband showed me, with trembling hands, the locket the first time — and when he crawled to me on his knees, begging for money to pay off this loathsome blackmailer, never knowing the blackmailer was me!"

"You are a liar, Mr. Collins," said Lady Ashe. "Perhaps he gave you money once, or even a second time. But my husband would never grovel before a man like you. There is nothing you could have told him that would make him do that."

"No? Then it appears you did not know your husband very well, Lady Ashe. All I had to do was threaten to kill you, and he was ready to give me everything in the world he possessed."

Charlotte heard, but she could not entirely comprehend. Only a day ago, she would have given this man her heart and her soul and have considered herself in heaven to be able to do so. Today she could only thank the kind Deity who had saved her from that madness.

Mr. Collins removed a pistol from his coat, which he pointed in the direction of Lady Ashe's heart. "This was a bonus I had not expected, making your acquaintance, Lady Ashe. It was touching to see how you tortured yourself over your husband's supposed infidelity, when all the time the only woman he ever truly cared about was you."

He came one step closer.

"I am sorry, Lady Ashe. Killing you was not part of my original plan. The story was to have ended in Brighton, at a little early morning duel. But your husband ruined everything. For some reason he decided to invite Lord March to join what was to have been a private party. And so after we left the gambling hell I accompanied Lord Ashe back to his rooms. He did not suspect a thing, until the moment I had my hands around his neck. After I strangled him, I slit his wrist and arranged his writing implements on the table, so his death would appear to be a suicide. Finding the piece of blotting paper in the writing box was a stroke of luck — Hopewell is a most comfortable house, as I believe you know, Lady Ashe — but in my haste I forgot to search for the locket, which was the one thing that might have connected me to the crime. The loss of the locket might not have mattered if that Bow Street Runner had not become involved — and if my wife had not tried to tell you my little secret that day on the moors. Yes, I am sorry, Lady Ashe. I truly am sorry you know too much. I enjoyed our little outing to Whitby. I might even write a poem about it, after you are dead."

He readied the pistol and prepared to fire. A shot rang out. A flock of gulls flew up to the sky, cawing like mad.

Theo Bryght came out from where he had been hiding.

"I beg your pardon, Ma'am," he said to Lady Ashe. "I hope I did not alarm you."

V.

It had not been easy to arrange a private meeting between Lady Ashe and Odelia Cunningham, but since the Runner disliked loose ends — he had mentioned it to everyone, several times — he bowed and begged his pardon until the two ladies found themselves sitting across a table in one of the inn's private rooms.

"There were two letters concerning Hopewell in the packet Lord Ashe sent me," the girl explained. "And there was this one."

Odelia gave the letter to Lady Ashe, who said, "You do not mind my reading it? The letter is addressed to you."

"I would have given it to you sooner, but ... my mother, Lady Cunningham, discovered the letters. She very much wished that I should marry Lord March, and so she thought it would be a good thing if you believed you had lost Hopewell, with the rest of your fortune, so you would leave Yorkshire. She was afraid Lord March might feel sorry for you and wish to make amends for what the family had done. He is not a bad man, Lady Ashe, just rather old."

Charlotte smiled. To a girl like Odelia, Lord March must seem positively ancient.

She then turned her attention to the letter — the letter she had searched for in Brighton but had not found because it had been addressed to Odelia Cunningham and put on the mail coach to Yorkshire while Lord Ashe was still alive.

Dearest Odious Odelia, she read, *I write this because you are the only person I have left in the world who I can hope still loves me. Your Uncle, whom you so mistakenly admire and believe to be a hero because he once fought Boney's frogs in Spain, has unfortunately landed on Queer Street and does not know how to get out.*

Truly, Odelia, I do not know if you shall ever see me again alive. If I do somehow escape from all this with my life and my honour intact, I will send word by the next mail coach. You will then please be so good as to destroy this letter, and the two letters that I have enclosed for Lady Ashe. But if you hear of my death, you must place the enclosed letters in Lady Ashe's hands directly and at once. It is very important that you do so, Odelia, so please find a way to be clever and do as I instruct.

I wish you much happiness. Perhaps one day, when you are married and sitting with a family of your own, you will recall the happy times we once had at Ramblewood, and remember

Your fond but foolish Uncle,
Ashe

Charlotte put the first letter aside and turned to the second one, which was addressed to her. Like the first letter, the seal had already been broken.

My dearest wife, if I may still address you by those words …

By the time you read this, I shall no longer be in this world and you will have learned that your fortune is lost. I have, though, found a way to keep Hopewell from the hands of the one who wished to destroy me, and, now that my life is over, my creditors. I have placed it in the temporary trust of Lord March — my instructions are in the second letter you will have received from my niece, Odelia. Give Lord March that letter, and show him this one as well, and tell him that I rely upon his honour to return Hopewell to you after the danger has passed. I will explain everything to him tonight, so he will know how to act to protect your interests.

I know I am not deserving of your forgiveness, just as I have not deserved either your love or your grandfather's trust. But I remain
Your faithful servant,
Ashe

Lady Ashe put this letter aside as well. The third letter — the transfer of ownership — she had already seen, and so she did not read it again.

"Thank you, Odelia," she said.

"Do you forgive me?"

Charlotte thought for a moment. If the girl had done as Lord Ashe had instructed, so much pain might have been avoided. Yet what possible good could come from holding a grudge, especially when Odelia was still only a child? The girl's first loyalty must be to her parents, even a parent such as Lady Cunningham.

And she did not want to hate. She did not want to hate the girl. She did not want to hate her husband. She wanted to remember him as he had been on the day they met at Ramblewood, when everything had seemed possible, including love.

And so she said, "Yes, Odelia, I do forgive you."

VI.

Lady March was anxious to return to Lundsmoor Park, and so arrangements were made to return the following day. First, though, Mr. and Mrs. Collins must be buried, and so a few of their party returned to the East Cliff, where the cemetery belonging to the parish church of St. Mary's was located.

They chose an hour when the sun was setting to escape the attention of curious townspeople, who had spoken of little else since the two tragedies had happened. Mrs. Seymour had begged Charlotte not to attend — it was enough that Lord March, Lord Lauferby, and the Runner would be there to pay their final respects. But Charlotte insisted on going, and so Mrs. Seymour accompanied her.

After the service, Charlotte drifted away from the group. She thought Lord March might wish for a few moments alone by the grave of Mrs. Collins. Apparently the others felt the same, since they also drifted away.

"You are looking for the grave of the sister?" asked Theo Bryght, who had come up beside her.

"Is it nearby?"

Theo Bryght accompanied her to the edge of the graveyard. "The key to the mystery was here, all the time," he said. Then he walked away.

The tombstone that marked the grave revealed that the girl's name had been Mary Collins. She had died when she was just sixteen. And, as the Runner had said, engraved on the tombstone were the words that explained the meaning of the locket, and all that had followed:

The wicked in his pride doth persecute the poor: let them be taken in the devices that they have imagined.

Charlotte placed a few flowers upon the grave and murmured a short prayer that the girl should now rest in peace. She then walked to the edge of the graveyard, where an iron fence stood guard, so that unsuspecting persons should not tumble off the cliff and fall into the sea. Flowers had been attached to some of the stakes.

"They are for those who were lost at sea."

Charlotte turned. An old woman was standing beside her. The woman had begun to take down a bunch of flowers that had wilted, intending to replace them with fresh ones.

"The sea took my husband in '74," the woman said as she did her work. "Since our loved ones have no grave except the sea, we widows tie our flowers of remembrance to this fence."

The woman glanced at Charlotte's black clothes. "Was your husband also lost at sea, my lady?"

Charlotte stared into the grey expanse. In the fading light, the distinction between water and sky had become blurred, until it seemed as though the entire world had melted into one vast, eternal mystery.

"No, not at sea — but lost, all the same."

CANTO THE SEVENTH

Theo Bryght placed his few belongings in his bag. He was not sorry to leave Lundsmoor Park, since the only person he cared to see again was leaving as well.

His window overlooked the lawn, and so he thought he might as well torture himself one last time. Lord March and Lady Ashe were seated on a bench. Perhaps the man was proposing to Lady Ashe at that very moment. Theo Bryght looked away.

But when the Runner entered the drawing room later, to give his thanks and say his good-byes, he was not greeted by the happy news of an upcoming marriage, which gave him hope.

"The carriage is here, Bryght," said Lord Lauferby, who had reentered the drawing room.

Good-byes were said again, and Lord Lauferby raced for the carriage. Theo Bryght was more than a little ashamed that his feelings were so very transparent that even Lauferby knew what was on his mind. But he was not displeased when Lady Ashe — and only Lady Ashe — accompanied him down the long hall and to the front door.

"I do not know how to thank you," she said.

He knew it was now his turn to say something, but he could think of nothing brilliant to say. And all the time they were taking step after step and soon they would be at the door and the opportunity would be gone.

"Be happy, Lady Ashe. That is all the thanks I need," he said at last.

"Happy? Yes, one day, perhaps."

They had reached the door.

"If you are ever in Yorkshire again, Mr. Bryght, I should be very happy to see you."

"Thank you, Lady Ashe. And if you are ever in London ... I hope you shall not need my services."

With that he ran out the door and into the waiting carriage.

II.

"I do not understand why you did not faint, Charlotte, when we were standing in the Abbey."

"I do not faint, Auntie. You know that."

"You might have made an exception, just this one time. A man often does not realize his true feelings about a woman until she faints."

Charlotte tried not to smile. She and Mrs. Seymour had left Lundsmoor Park — Ella had left before them, to help prepare Hopewell for their arrival — and their carriage had already reached the Hopewell moors. To the older woman's distress, they were returning to those moors without a firm proposal of marriage from Lord March.

Charlotte, however, was relieved. Too much had happened too quickly. She needed time to think. She had been mistaken about Lord Ashe. She had been mistaken about John Collins. She did not want to be mistaken again.

But now was not the time for serious thought, and so she said, casting a mischievous glance in the direction of her aunt, "I do not know if I wish to marry Lord March."

"Not wish to marry Lord March? Why in heaven would you refuse him?"

"For one thing, he was very much in love with poor Mrs. Collins. Think of the scandal. How will he ever live it down?"

"A man with his title and fortune? I think society will forgive him."

"There is also Mr. Bryght."

"Mr. Bryght? What on earth does he have to do with this conversation?"

"I think he is in love with me."

"The man would not dare to be so impertinent!"

"I wonder what it would be like to be the wife of a Bow Street Runner. With so much crime in London, it would surely never be dull."

"You cannot be seriously considering such a thing, Charlotte. And if you are, I blame it on all that poetry you read. If you continue to prattle on like this, I shall not let another word of that Lord Byron into the house!"

"Auntie—"

"Let me speak. I am not against an occasional verse. My first husband, Mr. George, wrote me a very nice sonnet when we became engaged."

"A sonnet? Auntie, I am shocked. I think I shall faint."

"You do not faint, Charlotte, remember?"

"But what is all this about Mr. George writing you poetry? You never mentioned that before."

"That is because it all happened so very long ago, and a person must be sensible and make the best of what life brings them, and when life brings you a Lord March you do not accept a Mr. Bryght instead. And ...

Charlotte, what are you doing? Why have you signaled to the coachman to stop?"

"Look, Auntie," said Charlotte, pointing to the distance, where a large house sat on top of a hill.

"Hopewell. Yes, I see it. But Charlotte .... Charlotte!"

Mrs. Seymour shouted after her niece, who had jumped down from the carriage and was running toward the summit.

"Charlotte! Where are you going?"

Charlotte turned back for a moment.

"Home!"

If you enjoyed this book, please let others know by leaving a review at your favorite online booksellers.
Thank you!

Enjoy These Other Books
By Jolie Beaumont:

What the Silk Mercer's Daughter Saw
A Theo Bryght, Runner Mystery
"A good clean mystery" - Amazon.com

In this new Regency mystery featuring Bow Street Runner Theo Bryght, he encounters not only dark passions and devastating secrets, but also a second chance to win the love of his life, Lady Charlotte Ashe.

Jericho's Child: A Cozy Regency Romance
"A good old fashioned Regency caper" - Romance Reviews Magazine

Sophie Moore has neither title nor fortune, but she hopes her talent for music will come to her aid, now that she is an orphan and must make her way in the world. But her practical plans are soon waylaid by a series of mishaps and misfortunes in the sparkling tradition of a cozy Regency romance.

Set for Murder: A Showbiz Is Murder Mystery

"Charming and suspenseful" – Amazon.com

It's the height of the Depression, but for Penny and Nick Garnett, two young Broadway stars about to make their London debut, life feels like one long musical comedy show — until a duchess is found murdered in her cabin. Who would want to murder the young and beautiful duchess? That's the question Scotland Yard Inspector Guy Travers must solve. When he begins to suspect an over-the-hill vaudeville performer, Penny and Nick rush to help their thespian friend. But with the ship now turned into a "set for murder," will they solve the mystery before the murderer comes back for a second act?

To find out more about these and future books, visit her website at
joliebeaumont.weebly.com